IN THE END

KEN SAIK

STRATTON
—PRESS—
Publishing Life

IN THE END
Copyright © 2021 **Ken Saik**

Stratton Press Publishing
831 N Tatnall Street Suite M #188,
Wilmington, DE 19801
www.stratton-press.com
1-888-323-7009

ISBN (Paperback): 978-1-64895-346-0
ISBN (Hardback): 978-1-64895-348-4
ISBN (Ebook): 978-1-64895-347-7

Printed in the United States of America

Note from author:

Did you enjoy reading In the End?

Your feedback helps me provide the best quality books and helps other readers like you discover great books.

Is there anything you find memorable about any of the characters or what they did or saw?

It would mean the world to me if you took two minutes to share your thoughts about this book as a review. You can leave a review on the retailer of your choice and/or send me an email with your honest feedback.

Do you know of anyone else for whom this book would be a good fit?

Thanks
Ken
My e-mail address is:
callingkensaik@gmail.com

ACKNOWLEDGMENTS

I am very thankful for the encouragement received from my grade school and high school teachers, which enabled me to never give up on my love for writing.

While the book took a backseat during most of my 31-year teaching career, my love for writing returned when I retired. Then I had the support of three beta readers who helped me keep my writing real and clear. Those fellow writers were Carl, Bathgate, Peggie Aspler and Royane Tomlyn.

CHAPTER 1

Sinkhole Swallows Twelve Teenagers

Two days in a row. A downpour.

Who cares? The attitude of Mr. Sanfield's son, Sampson, and eleven of his friends were partying in his two-car garage or, as they called it, their "man cave." On the third morning, the rain let up.

Mr. Sanfield tried to phone his son. Receiving no answer, he looked into his backyard, suspecting the boys were horsing around in the light rain. Through streams of water running down his window, he saw his garage had disappeared. His scream brought his wife. She confirmed the garage was gone.

Still in slippers, he raced out into the yard to a hole sixteen feet across and thirty feet wide. He dared to peer down into the dark abyss. He saw nothing. A cement section of the sidewalk shifted. He leaped to safety before it slid over the edge. From deep in the hole, he heard a crash. "The garage roof," he guessed. "That deep?"

"Sampson. Sampson," he screamed.

No answer.

Hoping the boys were somehow still alive in the garage, he raced to the house and called 911. His phone displayed two missed messages. Listening, he heard an appeal from a parent of one of Sampson's friends: "I can't raise my son on his cell. Is he okay?" The second message, another parent with the same request. Mr. Sampson chose to ignore the messages.

"Don't want to increase their concern," he said to his wife's questioning look. "I'll call when I know something more."

Guilt sat heavy on his shoulders. He opened the back door and stared out at the emptiness wishing there was something more he could do.

He felt responsible for the boys' disappearance. Why? He couldn't really say. Maybe it had something to do with Lenard Larson's father's phone call last night. He, too, had reported he couldn't reach his son. "Was everything alright?" Mr. Sampson had looked out the window and saw sheets of rain pelting down. A light in the garage window excused him from going out and getting soaked. "Your son's probably having too much fun to answer his phone," he told the father. He promised he'd check on them in the morning.

IN THE END

Now pacing the kitchen floor, Mr. Sanfield swore the fire department's arrival was taking too long. Blaming them was easier than second-guessing last night's decision—*I should've gone out and told them to come in.* Even though he saw no sign of trouble, he suspected they might be safer in the house.

He knew what their objections would be: "The garage is warm enough." "Out here we can be up as long as we want, be as loud as we want."

Anxious for some indication of the boy's survival, Mr. Sanfield, for the third time, headed toward the back door. He had to go, to call out to the boys again. Maybe he'd hear a response.

Three times his wife turned him back. The first time she screamed, "You can't leave me alone." The second time, she cried, the last time she ordered him back in, "It's too dangerous. You could be sucked into the hole too." That third time he'd already opened door. A first responder, Wossen, met him and seconded Mr. Sanfield's wife's concern. Wossen then went to the huge hole and began hammering metal poles in the ground and stretching a yellow Don't Cross tape.

The next half-hour tortured Mr. Sanfield. One of the responders asked him to note the names and home phone numbers of each of the boys in the garage. It diverted his attention. Mr. Sanfield did what he could and turned that request to his wife to complete. He continued to fume as he watched the responders standing around talking, planning maybe, but seemingly doing nothing. The first time

9

he challenged their actions, Wossen told him that help was on the way. The second time, after a chunk of the hole's circumference dived into the cavern, an older responder, Hammond, ordered him to stay in his house.

From his upstairs bedroom window, Mr. Sanfield watched the Pine Valley fire truck's hydraulically operated aerial ladder stretch out over the sink hole. Lights flooded the area. A harnessed fireman wearing an oxygen tank hung from a heavy cable. Holding a powerful light, he slowly descended. Then nothing.

Mr. Sanfield rushed downstairs and ran to the back door. Yanking it open, he found himself face-to-face with Hammond.

"We're in constant communication with Mr. Wossen, the rescuer who has been lowered to the garage roof. He's found an opening and will be trying to go in. As soon as there's something to report, we'll let you know." Hammond closed the door before Mr. Sanfield could object.

Back in his bedroom, Mr. Sanfield focused on the yellow five-foot markers attached to the cable that was being lowered into the backyard cavity. "They're searching," he guessed. "Progress." His eyes remained glued to the window. His wife came up and stood beside him.

"I should be down there," he whispered. "Sampson's my son." Looking at her, he added, "Our son." She wrapped her arm around his waist and held him tight, not wanting to lose both of the two most important men in her life.

At the first sign of the yellow cable markers moving up, Mr. Sanfield and his wife headed for the stairs. Then Mr. Sanfield raced back to the window thinking that he should count the markers. By the time he returned to the window, he knew he was too late. The markers were rising fast. He had no idea how many he missed, how deep the hole was.

Why up so fast? Something wrong? Did he find a boy? Mr. Sanfield raced after his wife. At the kitchen window, they watched the men unharness Wossen. He was alone. A police officer joined them.

"That's the third time," said Mr. Sanfield to his wife.

Wossen and Hammond had glanced three times at the parents standing in the window. Still no one took a step toward the house. Hammond pointed to the ladder. It began to retract. Wossen shook his head, pointed to the house, and shook his head again. More talking then three heads nodded.

"Good," said Mr. Sanfield when he saw Wossen turn and approach the house.

No sooner had Mrs. Sanfield opened the door than Dave Wossen introduced himself and declined the invitation to come inside. "I'm soaking wet and filthy."

"I'm sorry to have to say there was no sign of the boys anywhere in the garage," he began. "I had limited time and opportunity to move around, but I'm certain they were not there."

Turning to her husband, Mrs. Sanfield sobbed. He wrapped his arms around her. While patting her gently on the back, he turned to Dave Wossen.

"Start at the beginning. Tell me everything." Realizing he wasn't talking to one of his employees, he added, "Please."

"Yes, sir. My men lowered me to the roof of your garage. It was very slippery. The back's angled at forty-five degrees sloping down."

"How deep?"

"I don't know exactly, fifty, fifty-five feet. I didn't ask my men. The moment I touched the roof, the building lurched. I expected it to drop from my feet, but in a moment or two, it settled. That was my first warning. The position of the garage is very unstable. The twisted building resulted in a part of the roof jutting out. I attached a rope around a partial sheet of plywood then hooked it to the cable. When the men raised the cable, the plywood ripped away revealing a gaping hole. Best I could do. The men lowered me into the garage's interior. Twice my foot rested on a part of the building's structure. The creaking was so loud I pulled back immediately. From then on, I navigated around the garage while I was suspended."

"Did you call out for the boys?"

"I did, several times. No answer."

"Any sign of blood?"

"None that my light's beam could find."

"Go on."

"The most disturbing scene was about a quarter of the garage's back floor disappeared. Almost half of the rest of the floor sloped to the hole. Whatever was on that floor would have slid into the pit."

"So, no cots? No shuffleboard?

"Nothing."

"Pool table?"

"No."

"Wow! Must have been some hole."

"I'll tell you another thing. Your garage is not going to hang in that pit for very long. I had the men lower me down through it. Not very far, mind you. Just enough to get a look underneath the garage. Two slabs of rock are holding the front of the building and only one on the back. It's on this side that water trickles at a steady rate. It's eating away at the sand. Depending how far in the rocks are wedged in will determine how long the garage will stay where it is."

"What about the pit itself? Did you learn anything about that?"

"That was my last area of investigation. I told you about water trickling down from above the garage, but that was nothing compared to what I heard splashing below. I suspect there was at least one other source where water was pouring out. From the constant splashing, there has to be a fair amount of water, maybe even a small stream. I wanted to search the walls of the pit, but before I started the garage shifted and a brick fell. It took a long time before I heard it splash. At least I think I heard it hit water. I yanked a loose piece of wood from the wall of the garage and dropped it. I'm sure I heard it hit water. I forgot to count the seconds of its fall. So, you tried again?"

"I did, but I have to tell you something first. It's a responder's cardinal rule. If at any time we feel like we are in danger, we signal to be pulled out. Fair?"

"Yes."

"Well, I was tugging on a wet board. It didn't come loose. My hand slipped. I swung away. My cable scraped something above. The next thing I know, the whole garage starts shaking. I yelled, 'Up. Up.' The men hauled me up as fast as they could. I never got a chance to time another drop."

"From the one that you did hear, what would be your estimate of how long it took to hit water?"

Shaking his head, Dave said, "I'm guessing. . . five, maybe ten seconds. Could even have been fifteen. I can't really say. It took so long. I'm sorry."

"Don't be. You did all you could."

"Now, about that list of parents' contacts. If you have it handy, I'll take it and begin my phoning." Dave's hand reached out. "It's not a job I'm looking forward too, delivering such bad news."

Mrs. Sanfield left her husband's arms to go to the kitchen table for the list.

"If it is okay with you, I would like to call them. Family friends you know." He sidestepped to block his wife's return.

"Well, it is my job."

"And you just delegated to someone who can break the news most gently."

IN THE END

Mrs. Sanfield returned but stayed behind her husband, while Dave Wossen considered the suggestion. Relief eased the creases on his face. "Thanks. I really do appreciate your offer. I do have a report to file." He looked to his waiting men. A wave sent them boarding their truck. "Thanks again. I'll see you later."

After the men left, Mr. Sanfield scanned the list of names and phone numbers on the list that his wife brought. *That's the kids' names, not their parents. Lucky I'm doing the phoning.*

He paused at each name and pictured the face of each of Sampson's friends. Larry, Len, Graham, Terry, Conrad, Arny, Perry, Victor, Calvin, Brayden, Jean. *So many boys. So young. Gone before they could really enjoy life.*

He shook his head and looked at the list again. Seeing Jean's name, he thought of Gerald, Jean's father. *I'll call him last. He's real emotional. It may take time to calm him down.*

***

The death of twelve teenagers produced a flurry of activity in Pine Valley. Supportive phone calls from friends and family. Media interviews and arrangements for memorial services. As the week closes, grieving parents looked forward to a time to be by themselves, a time for peace and quiet.

Dave slowly approached Mr. Sanfield to express his condolences. His focus was redirected by Mrs.

Sanfield gently tugging on her husband's arm. Her concerned face and arm pointing to a man sitting in the corner by himself also caught Victor's father, Paul Nastrovich's attention.

For the last ten minutes, Ron Mastra, Perry's father, had been sitting by himself, face hidden in his hands. Occasionally, he slowly shook his head. Concerned Ron was crying, Mrs. Sanfield asked her husband to talk to him.

Before Stuart could answer, Paul lightly touched Stuart's arm and said, "Maybe I should go. I visited him earlier this week."

"If it is okay with you, I'd like to tag along. Just in case I might be of some help," said Stuart.

Mrs. Sanfield watched Dave and the two fathers weave their way around small clusters of people until Victor's mother approached her.

Ron hadn't noticed the arrival of the three men. Only when he heard Paul say, "Ron, you okay?" did he look up.

"Yeah." Ron's attention returned to the tiled floor.

Squatting, Stuart asked, "You sure?"

Paul matched Stuart's action.

Ron looked at his two friends, his eyes red. He paused and then said, "No."

"Care to talk about it?" Paul reached out and dragged a chair out from the wall. He sat in front of Ron. After a minute of silence, he added, "We're in this together, and together we can get through it."

Ron looked at Paul. "It's amazing. What strange things stick with you!"

Paul nodded.

"You know prayer was important to Perry." Ron's low voice forced the two fathers to learn closer to him.

"A value you taught him," said Paul.

"Modelled for him," added Stuart.

"He frequently thanked the Lord for his blessing. He often asked for the Lord's help when he faced a challenge. Nothing was too small for him to pray about."

"And he prayed for his friends too," added Paul, remembering when Perry prayed for him and Victor two summers ago.

"But in such a terrifying situation, would he have turned to the Lord? I wish I was there to see him pray. Then I would know he wouldn't have been afraid. If only I could've seen that..."

Paul shoved his chair beside his friend and wrapped his arm around his shoulder.

"We raised our children well. Count on that. Habits kick in. Maybe not immediately, but they do. Believe me."

"But in such an emergency?"

"I've learned that in any situation. Remember when Victor joined the Reserves?"

"The Canadian Armed Forces?"

"Yes. Victor was gone for so long. Don't get me wrong. The training, the fitness, all good, but it felt like he was abandoning our community. I couldn't understand how he could do that. He missed the Young Adults summer camp. He and his friends always looked forward to working with the handicapped children. Later, he admitted he made a mistake. The following year, he signed up for the summer camp. The value of friends and helping the community returned. In the same way, even if Perry is momentarily sidetracked by being trapped in the garage, his base value will return."

"But until he admitted that he made a mistake, weren't you worried?"

"For sure. That's how I learned that I had to count on Victor following what my wife and I taught him. That is the hope that we have to rest on."

"Paul's right," said Stuart, standing up.

Ron nodded. Paul mouthed, "I'll stay with him."

As Mr. Sanfield and Dave walked away, Stuart said in a low voice, "I think he'll be okay, at least for a while."

"And how about yourself? How are you doing, sir?" asked Dave after expressing his condolences and shaking Mr. Sanfield's hand.

"Please, call me Stuart."

"As you wish."

"Thankfully, I've been keeping my feelings in check, but it's been a hectic week making arrangements," began Sanfield. He shook his head, not wanting to air emotional details of preparing for the funeral services. Reporters phoning or knocking at our door." He recalled Mrs. Sanfield crying during two of the interviews. "You know we had to hunt around for a place to rent. I had to move out of my house."

"I expected that."

"There was another cave-in. Can you believe that? The cavity in my yard is at least twenty-five feet wider. The garage is gone."

Dave nodded.

Ralph Hawthorn, Conrad's father, and Gerald Ross, Jean's father, approached. Arthur Housma, Terry's father, came up and wrapped his arm around Mr. Sanfield.

"Thank God for friends like Ralph here." Mr. Sanfield nodded to his right. "You know none of this seems real. It happened in my own backyard, and yet I still can't believe it." A tear crept out from the corner of his eye. He wiped it away. "Losing all those boys. It's such a huge shock."

"For us it is too," added Ralph, squeezing his friend. "I've been praying that the Lord will comfort us."

"Me too," said Mr. Sanfield

"I'm trying to accept what the priest said. For the boys, it's a blessing. Our sons are in heaven with God."

"You've got to be kidding. What kind of comfort is that?"

Gerald's outrage caused Ralph to take a step back. In a lower voice, he said, "I only meant—"

"We know what you mean, Ralph," said Mr. Sanfield. "But at this moment, our feelings of loss overwhelm our knowledge of our boy's blessing." A gentle tug on Stuart's arm redirects his attention.

"I'll never see Jean get married, have children, graduate from—"

Stuart's arm reached around Gerald and gave him a light hug. In a normal tone, he said, "Coping with our loss will be very hard. When the ones you've grown to know and love, aren't around anymore, how do you handle that? I know it's really helped me to have all those calls and visits over this last week."

"That's not uncommon," said Dave. "You probably see the parents of the tragedy coming together and supporting each other like they never have before. It's not uncommon."

"Now that's a blessing," said Gerald. "

"For sure," added Mr. Sanfield.

"They're joined by Rick Lambert, Arny's father. After Dave shook his hand and offered his condolences, Rick said, "So I imagine this event wraps up all your work here. No loose ends, I'll bet."

Dave nodded and stepped back as friends of Ross and John approach. Mr. Sanfield observed a look of concern on Dave's face.

"Something wrong?" he asked. Dave led them away from the group growing around John and Ross.

"Not really." The frown remained on Dave's face.

"But?"

"It's something Ross said." Dave debated whether he should share one little omitted fact.

"Yes." Mr. Sanfield adjusted his body, so he stood square in front of Dave, blocking an escape.

"Loose ends," Dave began. "When I was hanging below the garage pulling on that last stubborn board, a long rope hit me in the face. A loose rope. That's why I lost my grip. I had to shove it away. Now I can't help wondering why it was hanging below the garage. As I was being pulled up, I recall seeing the rope tied to a beam. Tied not just hanging, a deliberate action. Why?"

CHAPTER 2

In the Cavity

A chorus of "heys" erupted after three boys were thrown from their cots in the dark two-car garage. Calvin and Len scrambled for the light switch.

"Lights are out," shouted Calvin over the chaos of "What happened? What's going on? Hey! Watch it."

Seconds later, Brayden's voice rose above expressions of frustration and confusion. "I'll get a light."

Brayden, a semi-reformed smoker, withdrew a lighter and flicked it on. A habitual motion drew his hand to his mouth as if to light up. He'd refused to throw the needless object away to demonstrate he had conquered the habit.

"Flashlights are in the cupboard," shouted Sampson Sanfield as his feet carefully poked their way on the cement to the front of the garage.

Brayden reached the cupboard first. He groped inside, grabbed one flashlight, and shone a path for

Sampson. Then he handed a second flashlight to Sampson.

Two light beams probed the garage's inky interior. The dust particle beams exposed half-empty shelves, golf awards, and camping lanterns dangling on the wall.

"Oh shit," a reaction from the two boys.

They'd exposed several large jagged breaks in the drywall. The exploring spotlights discovered a broken box of poker chips and two boxed decks of cards on the cement floor beneath a shelf. Closer to the back door, a toppled golf bag leaned against two rolled-up sleeping bags. Two of Sampson's four water guns lay spilled on the floor near the bags.

Sampson's beam found two red snooker balls sitting beyond the water guns. In a flash, his light shot to the wall on the opposite side of the garage. Half the red balls were no longer in the rack. Brayden's light joined Sampson's and began scouting around on the floor. Three balls had rolled up to the couch where Terry had been sleeping.

"Terry, don't move."

Brayden's warning froze Terry with one bare foot still in the air above broken glass. An empty beer glass had fallen from the nightstand by the couch. Sampson's light skated around the couch until it found Terry's sandals. After Terry backed away, he put on his sandals. Sampson's light slid along the floor finding two more snooker balls. Brayden's light joined Sampson's in time to spot a narrow crack in the cement. It widened as it angled to the center of the garage's back door. Together they followed the deepening crevice. The depression increased rapidly. At its lowest point, the floor dropped almost half a foot below the bottom of the closed overhead door.

Victor's shuffling feet neared Sampson. He leaned close to his friend and whispered, "Think there was an earthquake?"

"Don't know," responded Sampson. "But I'd like to see what's outside."

Looking at a water bottle that had rolled into the middle of the floor's depression, he stepped forward. One, two, three steps. The littered floor sagged. The lower walls groaned from the tugging pressure of the moving floor.

Victor's heavy hand yanked Sampson back. "What are you doing?"

Victor's serious voice caused Sampson to shine the light on his friend's face. His long black hair looked like it lost a fight with the pillow.

Victor waved the light down and said, "Didn't you feel the floor dropping?"

"No."

"Well, it did. I saw the depression sink at least an inch." He pointed to the floor's lowest level under the overhead door."

Sampson saw no difference, shrugged his shoulders, and said, "I just wanted to look under the door. See what's outside. "

"Then walk along the side of the garage." He pointed to the section of the floor that hadn't dipped. "And when you get to the door, don't walk out there.

We've no idea what is holding this floor up. Lie down, like when a person who fell through the ice is being rescued."

Sampson followed his friend's advice as if he were at St. Peter's summer camp for disadvantaged kids. There Victor was in charge of the Young Adults councillors. Last year, Sampson had volunteered as a counselor.

Sampson stretched out on the cold floor and began sliding toward the opening under the door. On the other side of the garage, Brayden did the same. Victor squatted beside Sampson's ankles, prepared to grab them if the floor gave way. Seeing no one at Brayden's feet, he looked back at the other boys. He pointed to Brayden and then at Arny.

"Just in case." Victor's voice wasn't very loud, but his sharp hand motion commanded a response. He and Arny worked for the same landscaper. Victor was Arny's supervisor. He'd worked for the landscaper for two more years than Arny.

Sampson's forehead touched the cold floor. His light stabbed the darkness beyond the opening. Twice Sampson's light swept left and then right. He said nothing. All the boys strained their ears hoping for some kind of news.

Brayden positioned himself opposite Sampson. "Can I help?" he asked hoarsely.

"Shine your light where mine is," Sampson said without taking his eyes from the unknown. Their lights arced left and right. "It's like we have a black curtain blocking our view. Like there's nothing out there. What do you think?"

"Hey, guys. What's out there? Out with it." Arny's request echoed several of the other boys' mutterings.

Brayden and Sampson wiggled their way from the opening and looked at anxious faces.

"Don't know," began Sampson. He glanced at Brayden who nodded in agreement.

"Louder," yelled Terry.

"It's like there's nothing out there. I can't see the neighbor's garage across the lane. Not even the fence on either side."

"There's some kind of textured surface out there. If I didn't know better, I'd say we're buried alive," added Brayden.

His comment unleashed a loud outburst. "Whoa! Wow! What? You kidding?"

Sampson waved both his arms for attention. His light raced back and forth across the ceiling. "Whatever it is," said Sampson when he finally regained their attention, "I think that surface isn't that close. We can barely make out what's outside these walls. Too dark. Can't tell how far anything is." Fearing he lost his ability to judge distance, Sampson's light slid around the interior of the garage to satisfy himself that he could still judge distance.

"Think you can squeeze through that opening to get a look outside of this door?" asked Arny, pointing to the space beneath the metal door. The tone of his voice was for Brayden and Sampson to hear.

"Good idea," added Victor. "Slide out as far as you dare. I'll hang on to your feet."

"I was thinking of that," said Sampson as he squatted down. The floor vibrated. Brayden matched his friend's movement only in slow motion. He didn't voice his fear.

Several boys sounded their approval and watched Sampson poke his head beyond the garage's interior. His shoulders prevented more progress. With the flashlight pressed tight against his side, Sampson searched the area outside the garage.

Silence gripped the boys as if they waited for a new report.

"Well?" asked Victor in a voice that sounded too loud the moment the word hit his ears.

"This isn't working."

"Want me to pull you back?" Victor took hold of both of Sampson's ankles.

His tight grip triggered a memory, a time when Sampson observed Victor's hand turn red clutching a ladder. At that time, Arny had neared the top of a ladder to pick some large apples at Victor's father's place. The top branches waved. The ladder leaned to the side, but Victor's grip held.

A comforting thought flashed across Sampson's mind. *No way he loses his grip.*

"Sampson?" Victor's call refocused Sampson. "Want me to pull you back?"

"No. No."

The conviction of Sampson's response caused Victor to ease his hold.

"Make this opening bigger so I can force my shoulders through."

"How?" Brayden's wrinkled forehead looked to Victor for a suggestion.

"Figure it out." Annoyed, Sampson shook his head.

"That's okay. I've got it," shouted Victor for Sampson's benefit. He looked into the garage's dark interior and called for Graham, a short but agile 220-pound boy, the heaviest guy in the garage.

"Yeah," came a skeptical response from the darkness.

The boys stepped aside, allowing Graham to come forward. Brayden's light picked him out of the group.

"I want you to walk slowly toward Sampson." As Graham angled his way toward Victor, Victor said, "No."

Graham stopped immediately as if he'd been about to do something dangerous.

"Follow the crack in the floor to Sampson. When the floor sinks, he can squeeze out farther."

"I don't know. What if it collapses?"

"Don't worry. Arny'll grab Brayden's feet, and I'll get Sampson's."

"What about me?"

"You'll have plenty of time to jump to safety," said Arny.

In response to the disgust in Arny's, voice Graham stepped back.

"Brayden," said Arny, "shine your light on the wall near the clubs. I think I saw a rope hanging there." Arny's eyes shifted to Len.

Len nodded. His feet began sliding in the direction Arny indicated. Brayden's beam flew to the wall, located the rope, and guided a path through scattered items for Len.

Hurrying, Len gave Graham the rope. "Tie it to your waist or just hang on. We'll have the other end." He pointed to their friends behind him.

Hanging on to the rope Graham inched his way to the garage door. The opening dropped but not enough for Sampson to squeeze under the door. Following Len's direction, Calvin, Len's close friend, shuffled up beside Graham.

The floor sank from the added weight. Sampson wiggled halfway out bringing the flashlight too. Once the belt on Sampson's pants disappeared out of the garage, Victor took firm hold of Sampson's ankles. Sampson twisted one way, then another. Brayden's hand reached around Sampson. Even though he couldn't see much outside, he aimed his light in the same direction as Sampson did. The boys in the garage focused on the two bodies lying on the floor. Ears anxiously waited for news.

After four long minutes, an involuntary, "Oh no" escaped Sampson's mouth. He knew he'd spoken too loudly when he heard a concerned "What?" from both Arny and Brayden. He clamped his mouth shut, determined to say nothing more until they hauled him back. His exploration continued until his back muscles complained.

At Sampson's request, Victor dragged Sampson back into the garage. Sampson walked away from the floor's depression. The boys followed. Sampson turned, faced his friends, and shook his head. With Brayden's light focused on Sampson's chest Sampson said, "It's not good. I think we're stuck in a hole, kind of." He let the news take root, figuring what to report next, when to break the worst news.

After few moments of silence, Victor said, "Kind of?"

"What kind of hole?" Graham stepped closer to hear better.

"Louder," said a voice from the back of the boys.

"Deep. Very deep. My light couldn't find the bottom."

"A hole like one in a volcano, a dormant one?" Graham glanced to the right for a reaction from Arny. Arny's eyes widened at his friend's comparison.

"Yes. The hole's deep, and wide, but it sounds like there's water at the bottom. In fact, water is streaming down most of the sides of the hole."

"So, like water running down the side of the mountain?" ventured Graham with more confidence. He smiled, capturing the image in his mind, thinking of last year's camping trip the group took.

"Not that much water, but it's doing the same thing, carving dirt from the sides, making a larger hole. And that's where I see trouble."

"Then the rocks on the side of the hole must be sandstone," said Graham.

"Or some other soft rock. The running water has cut deep crevices, about a foot deep I'd say. And the crevices run down as far as I can see."

"Can't be that serious," added Graham. "The erosion you described takes years, not hours to wear away. Even with all the rain that we've had in the last couple of days, I think we have nothing to worry about." He shook his head and looked to Arny. Arny nodded smiling.

"If it were the sides of the wall that were pinching us in place, but I don't think that is what is preventing the garage from falling father."

"What do you mean?" asked Arny, his face serious again. Graham turned and shuffled closer to better hear Sampson.

"You know the thin metal tabs that hold the backing in a picture frame?

"Yeah." His forehead furrowed.

"There's three rocks on the sides holding the garage up. One large flat rock." He pointed to the side of the garage where the rope hung. "And from what I could see, two on the other side. I bent down so far I was afraid I was going to drop into the hole." He looked to Victor. "I wouldn't even have tried to look under the floor if I couldn't feel your hands on my ankles. Thanks."

"Glad I helped. I actually thought I was wasting my time." Victor smiled and looked around to see that the other boys heard the compliment.

"Guys, hold on." Graham waited for attention. "You don't know if there are any more pins like that toward the front of the garage?"

"No."

"And you don't know if the pins, or tabs if you want, are say, 80 percent stuck into the wall or only 50 percent?"

"Right. And if they're only 50 percent it won't take much for the water to loosen those rocks. And let me tell you the rainwater is still pouring down from above. Those rocks could give away at any moment. Then we'll go crashing down. If this hole doesn't narrow so we get wedged in again, we'll fall into the water. I don't know how deep that water is, but I sure hope you can swim." The pitch in his voice rose with the speed of the words.

In a much calmer tone, Arny and Graham indicated swimming would be no problem. Several other boys echo the response.

"Well, I don't swim." Brayden's response came across as if he was objecting to a marathon swim.

"Really!" Len elbowed Larry.

The boys knew that Brayden didn't have an ounce of athlete blood in him. Like Graham, he was heavy and short; but unlike Graham, his movements were slow. He was happiest playing pool, cards, and video games. At times like that, Sampson always made sure that Brayden was invited to the party.

Ignoring Len's mocking surprise, Brayden said, "Yes. I dropped out of phys ed when I heard that swimming was part of the program. You remember."

He controlled the anger in his voice, but his face turned red, something Len missed in the dark.

"Afraid of the water?" Len laughed and nudged Larry who half snickered.

"And what of it?" snapped Brayden.

"Mother tried to drown you when you were little?" gibed Larry laughing. Len joined in.

"Guys. Guys. Cut it out." Sampson overrode their teasing. "This is serious. We have to figure out how to get out of here."

Victor placed a hand on Larry's shoulder, leaned closer to his ear, and whispered, "Larry, we don't treat our friends that way."

Larry turned, saw Victor's serious face, and nodded. He looked to Brayden and apologized.

Arny raised his voice. Once he had their attention, he suggested that they look at climbing up to get out of the hole. He admitted that he didn't know how far they would have to climb, but he thought it was an option.

CHAPTER 3

A Hope

Calvin volunteered to go up on the roof of the garage and check out how far they had to climb. Seeing his red soccer cap on the floor, he scooped it up and placed it firmly on his head, visor pointing back. The cap had been given to him and his soccer team after they won the city's first annual Pine Valley tournament. After that victory, he always wore the cap.

"Wait a minute, guys. Wait a minute," Sampson yelled. Everyone stopped. "There's one more thing." He waited until everyone quit moving. "Before I asked to be pulled in, I checked the floor I was lying on, the buckled part. The rebar in the cement is loose. Nothing is holding it. With a little pressure the floor in that area will cave in."

"Then it really was necessary for us to hang on to your ankles," said Arny.

"No. If the floor caved in, Brayden and I would have fallen in the hole and dragged you guys down with us. That's why after Victor dragged me back in here, I headed for this spot. We need to keep away from that section of the floor."

Calvin asked for someone to bring the eight-foot stepladder hanging on a pair of hooks at the front of the garage so he could get into the attic. Arny repeated Sampson's warning and directed Brayden to shine a light to the step ladder. He grabbed a third flashlight from the cupboard, and in less than five minutes, he and Calvin were stepping on the ceiling's rafters. They made their way to the front of the garage where Calvin kicked the air vent out.

The moment he stuck his head out he shouted, "Hey, it's pouring out here."

While Calvin examined the best way to reach the roof, Sampson stepped up on to the attic. Len and Larry followed him up the ladder.

Calvin wiggled his way back into the attic. With water dripping off his face, he said, "Need a shovel to widen a spot."

"Shovel?" asked Sampson.

"The wall is hard sand, but I should be able to chip away at it to get to the top." He shook his head. He'd considered asking for his jacket that was piled in a heap by the garage's front door, but he figured he was already soaked.

"Shovel," yelled Len as he climbed into the attic.

The request was repeated, and a shovel was passed up to Larry who had remained at the top of the ladder. He forwarded it to Len. Calvin received the shovel and squeezed through the vent. He hacked away at the wall near the peak of the roof. Arny and Len poked their heads through the vent to watch Calvin's progress while Sampson called down for his jacket. Larry echoed the request.

By the time Larry and Sampson put their jackets on and picked their way over the rafters to the vent, Calvin had handed the shovel back to Arny. He then hauled his body up to the roof. In school, he'd spent much of his time in the weight lifting room. Arny gave Calvin his flashlight and accepted Calvin's hand up. After Sampson passed his light up, Arny helped him up to the roof. In turn, Sampson did the same for Len and Larry.

Sampson pointed his light to where Arny and Calvin were standing, planning how they might scale up the side of the hole. He joined his friends.

"So, what do you think?" asked Sampson.

Calvin shined a beam of light on many rocks imbedded in the hole's wall. "Possible. As long as we can find grips. It's wet. Won't be like wall climbing in gym."

"Unfortunately, from here we can only see about a third of the way up," added Arny. He wiped the water from his face.

Calvin turned the flashlight off. "In the dark, it looks like we can see about five feet away. Should be far enough to pick our way up." He handed the flashlight back to Arny.

"Let's see how well that works." Calvin snugged his cap down. Using a few protruding rocks for toeholds and hand grips, Calvin picked his way up. One foot, two feet, three feet. He looked down. "Easy."

"And what happens if you get to the top?" asked Len.

"Go for help," responded Calvin without hesitation.

"Which could take some time. The garage could be at the bottom of the hole by then," added Sampson.

"You got some ropes?" asked Arny.

"Yeah."

"Then we'll carry them up, lower the ropes down, and pull you guys up. Don't worry, Sampson, we'll get out of here one way or another."

Arny returned to the point on the roof where he climbed up and hollered for the ropes. Brayden, who had perched himself on the rafter above the stepladder, forwarded Arny's request. Arny sat on the peak of the roof and watched the beam from Sampson's light.

He's found something else wrong, thought Arny when he saw the light remain on a few stepholds. *Sampson always picks out obstacles.*

At first Arny felt annoyed that Sampson could be such a stumbling block for his ideas. When he thought of the ropes, he changed his mind. *Could be a good thing,* he concluded in reference to Sampson's critical eye.

After Brayden passed the ropes up to Arny, Arny joined his friends at the other end of the garage.

"See that?" asked Sampson, pointing to a round rock dripping with water.

"Yeah," answered Arny.

"Wet. Smooth. Easy to slip from. Something like that could cause you to come crashing down." Sampson redirected the flashlight at Arny. He saw no concern on Arny's face.

"You saying we shouldn't try?" asked Arny in disbelief.

Calvin turned Sampson to face him. "I hope not. We really don't have any choice. Stay here and we'll likely die at the bottom of this hole. Climb out and we have a chance to survive. At least we're doing something."

Arny faced Sampson. "He's right you know."

Nodding, Sampson said, "I know. I know. I just don't want to see you guys hurt."

Thanks," said Calvin.

"You know, Sampson," said Arny, "if you try just a little harder, you could sound just like my mother." He laughed, slapped him on the shoulder, and turned to Calvin. "Shall we?" He handed his flashlight to Len.

Calvin took one of the two coils of twenty-five-foot ropes from Arny and tossed it over his shoulder. "No time like the present."

They both walked to the edge of the hole, whispered a few words, and began picking their way up. After going up three feet, Calvin reached over and touched Arny's shoulder. "Race you to the top."

Sampson's light beam focused on Calvin's head. "Guys, that's not funny."

Both Arny and Calvin looked down and unison said, "We know. This is serious." Laughter followed. The next four-foot ascent happened without incident. Then a rock that Arny hoped to pull himself up with pulled free from the wall and dropped. He heard it strike the roof. When he looked down, Len, Larry, and Sampson were stepping back from the wall.

"Sorry," Arny called out.

At about twelve feet, Sampson noted that both Arny and Calvin needed the same rock to move higher. They took turns. Sampson prayed the rock would hold. It did. The farther up the two boys climbed, the harder it was for Sampson and Len to see what their climbers were grabbing. When they saw Calvin pull what they presumed to be a pocketknife from his pants, they thought he was carving a larger hole for a grip. Falling sand confirmed their assumption. Somewhere higher up, Sampson could only see the back of Calvin's white runners. At times, no movement took place. Calvin was about three feet higher than Arny when Sampson heard Arny's "shit."

"What happened?" screamed Sampson.

All they heard was "my eyes."

"Sand in Arny's eyes," guessed Len. "He was looking up. Sand came loose from Calvin's last hold."

A moment later, Arny's "oh, no," pierced the dark. The crack of a loose rock hit the roof, then Arny's body pounded the shingles. Len's light flashed to Arny's landing point. At first it appeared as if Arny attempted to roll to spread the impact on his body. Then Len realized Arny was sliding to edge of the roof. The rope flew from his grip.

"Watch out, Arny," yelled Len. He shoved the flashlight into Larry's belly and scrambled to catch a hold on his friend. Sampson's light directed his path.

A second crashing sound.

Calvin, thought Sampson.

Larry rushed to his aid, but Calvin landed like a cat. His hands and feet stabilized his body on the gritty, wet, sloped surface.

"Hurry," shouted Sampson as he saw Arny's rope disappear over the edge of the roof. Len was less than a foot away.

A scream shot from Arny's mouth seconds before Len grabbed his collar and then his arm. Arny had jammed his feet into the sandy wall for a brace to prevent him from going over the edge. The right foot twisted slightly after striking a rock that refused to budge.

Relief from the boy's fall was brief. Calvin noticed the garage's descent first. Their side of the garage slid down an inch or two then another two inches. The drop increased to a foot in a couple seconds, then four feet. Screams from inside and outside the garage pierced the air. Then the fall stopped. Silence opened the door for thank-god prayers, but only for a minute. A sound like two trucks hitting each other filled the air. The next instant, the garage dropped again, faster than Sampson had time to estimate the distance they fell. From inside the garage came screams of terror mixed with the sound of things banging into each other.

Like objects dropped into an empty dumpster from a front-end loader, thought Sampson.

The building shuddered. The boys didn't move for fear of starting another fall.

Slowly, Arny pulled the bottom of his white T-shirt up to wipe his face. Sampson's light traced Arny's movement. Smeared blood covered the bottom of his wet shirt. Using a different part of his shirt, Arny wiped his forehead again. More blood.

"Let me," said Sampson. He hastened to his friend's side. Shining the light on Arny's face, he used part of the T-shirt to gently dab Arny's cheekbone. "Just a nasty scrape."

Directing Sampson's light, Arny examined the rest of his body. A major rip on the right knee of his new jeans, beneath a bloodstain from where the knee scraped the shingles. He pulled his leg up, and using an unstained portion of his shirt, he wiped the blood and grit from the wound.

"Guys, you have to see this." Calvin pulled his head away from a piece of plywood that he'd torn away from the roof. He held the flashlight he taken from Len.

Len and Larry each grabbed a sheet of plywood and pulled so they could look down into the garage. As Calvin backed away from the hole in the roof, Len took a firmer grip of the plywood. Larry kneeled down and poked his head into the garage. Calvin aimed the light into the darkness below.

"Wow!"

"What?" asked Len.

"The floor. It's gone." Larry started to back away from the hole as Sampson approached.

"Not all of it," corrected Calvin. To help Len, Calvin took hold of the sheet of plywood that Len was struggling with. His hand missed being jabbed by two nails.

"What about the guys?" asked Sampson. He was on his knees waiting for Larry to make room for him to look into the garage.

Victor was shining Calvin's flashlight in the garage. He told Calvin that everyone appeared okay except for Brayden. He'd been on the stepladder when the building dropped. Brayden took a tumble, was a little banged up, but okay. Victor's report didn't stop Sampson from shining his light into the scene below.

Pulling himself from the hole in the roof, Sampson said, "We'd better get down there fast. I've got to check something out."

"Squeezing through this," said Larry, "isn't an option". Pointing to the other far end of the garage, he added, "Better return the way we came." He stood up and edged himself to the escape spot. The boys followed his lead, Arny last, favoring his injured right foot.

Calvin waited for Arny. "I'll lower you down, so you don't hurt your foot anymore."

Arny nodded. Using only the strength of his arms, Calvin lowered Arny. Then he eased himself down. Larry, Len, and then Sampson wiggled their way down to the garage vent opening. Victor dropped the light down to Larry and them.

Sampson delayed long enough to assure himself that Arny needed no extra assistance. Then he started after Len, who was feeling his way to the attic entrance hole. Using his foot, Len swept away the pink insulation to expose the ceiling joists. Uncertain if the large boards would still support him, he set his foot down then slowly transferred his weight to the forward foot.

Sampson showed no hesitation. With one hand against the inside roof to keep his balance and the other clutching the flashlight, he hunched past Len, reached the attic opening, and called for someone to bring the step ladder.

A muffled "I'll get it," and then the dragging of the metal stepladder reached Sampson's ears. Soon the top of the step ladder appeared, too far for Sampson to step on. From Larry's light Sampson guessed he saw Conrad and Brayden bend over and pull some objects across the floor.

"Is the ladder here?" asked Len, pointing down. Without waiting for a response, he pressed his hand against the top of his head. Water dripped down his forehead and into his eyes. Len began to lose his balance. Sampson's hand shot out and steadied him.

The scraping of the ladder's legs on the cement pulled both boys' attention to the action below.

"Won't be long now," said Sampson.

Sampson handed his flashlight to Len. He aimed his feet for the ladder's top step. His foot kicked the ladder, but Conrad caught it before it fell. With Brayden standing on the bottom step, Sampson secured a safe footing. He took his flashlight back and descended.

"You okay?" asked Sampson after stepping back from the ladder. He directed his light to Brayden's face and saw a deep cut across his friend's right cheek. More searching revealed a jagged rip in Brayden's short sleeve blue sweater.

"Sore. Nothing serious," said Brayden with a shrug.

The ladder jumped. Brayden and Sampson reached out, but Conrad had already steadied the ladder. Graham joined the boys. He too carried a flashlight, the last one that was stored in the cupboard at the front of the garage.

"Not as easy as I thought," said Len with a laugh after he found his footing.

"You good here?" asked Sampson, looking at Conrad. He nodded. Sampson checked with Graham to confirm there was no problem.

"What's up?" Brayden hurried to catch up with his friend.

Sampson's mission-pace changed to a slow-motion approach. *That big!* As Sampson neared the gaping hole in the garage floor, he squatted down and aimed his light to the outside wall searching for the stream of water that he saw reflected when he first peered into the hole.

"There," he announced with excitement, pointing to the wall several feet below the garage's floor. "Doesn't that look like an opening, a tunnel in the wall maybe?"

Brayden aimed his light where Sampson's light focused, but the distance was too great to provide a clear indication as to the size of the opening in the wall.

"Could be." Brayden's voice lacked conviction. "Any other spots like that?" His light began exploring the wall while Sampson's remained.

"What you looking at?" Victor squatted beside the two boys.

Calvin, standing a few feet away, said, "This place gutted or what?" He glanced around again in disbelief.

"What looks like a hole in the wall," answered Sampson. He looked to Victor to read a facial reaction but saw none.

Victor bent forward for a better look and said, "A possible escape route?"

"Hey! I like that!" Calvin accepted their description as fact, then took Larry's light and added it to the spot of interest.

"Can't tell much from here," said Len who arrived with Larry.

"Gotta go down and take a look. Make sure it's a tunnel." Calvin shrugged, indicating his statement was a no-brainer.

"It has to be a tunnel. The flow of water must have cut some kind of path." Sampson's nod showed he had the same thought as Brayden.

"But is it large enough for us to crawl through?" asked Victor.

"Only one way to find out." Calvin looked around to see that everyone was waiting for him to finish. "It's obvious. Someone's gotta go down there."

"Calling Spider-Man. Calling Spider-Man." Len laughed and nudged Larry who followed suit. "Anyone up for the job?"

"I am."

Everyone looked at Calvin.

"You serious?" Larry's tone indicated he'd never risk his neck for such a venture.

"Absolutely." Silence greeted Calvin's answer. "Got an extra rope?" Calvin looked to Sampson.

"Left cupboard at the front," answered Sampson.

"Just in case the drop is more than it looks."

Calvin explained that the two ropes would be tied together, then looped over a bent but reinforced beam stretching across the back of the garage. A loop at one end of the rope would permit Calvin to put his foot in it.

"Then you guys can lower me down. I'll take a light with me so I can shine it directly into the hole. Simple."

"Assuming you aren't too heavy for us," said the 220-pound Graham. A couple boys patted Graham on his back for the shot at his friend.

As soon as the laughter died down, Calvin said, "You should talk." At his heaviest, Calvin once weighed 160.

"Then it's decided," said Arny over the excited chatter. "Calvin's going down to see if we have a way out of here." Shouts of approval rang out. "I just want you all to know if it wasn't for this bum foot I would have volunteered to go down." He shook his foot and faked a frown. Amidst the laughter, Len volunteered to get the other rope.

Conrad's voice cut through the merriment. His tone demanded a moment of seriousness. "Calvin's risking his life out there. We can't take any chances." He backed his concern by questioning if the beam that Calvin referred to could hold his weight. If so, for how long? How long could Calvin stand with his foot in the rope's loop?

At his direction, they set up the extension ladder over the expanse where Calvin would be lowered. If the beam started to give way, Calvin would have time to escape. They also timed Calvin to see how long he could stand on one foot. Graham and Brayden each grabbed the rope and hung on to it for five minutes to check if the beam showed any sign of stress.

With preparations complete, the boys gathered together. The usually mouse-quiet Perry asked for silence. He suggested they pray. Calvin noticed a frown creep on to Brayden and Jean's face. After a brief moment, Calvin stepped up beside Perry and thanked him. After the prayer, he looked at the two skeptics and said that if they prayed first before attempting to climb up, then maybe Arny wouldn't have wrecked his foot.

Len, Larry, Graham, and Jean volunteered to lower Calvin, then added as if an after-thought, and to bring him back up again. When the laughter died down, the boys picked up their end of the rope, and Calvin took his.

Arny called for a time-out. With a grin, he approached the four work-horse boys and asked if any held any kind of grudge against Calvin. "Just making sure that my buddy comes back safely," he said in response to the groans of a couple of his friends. A seriousness crossed Arny's face as he approached Calvin.

"My dear, wonderful buddy. I do have an extra apology to make to you before you go down, there."

"Extra apology?"

"About a dirty trick I tried to pull on you. But first a question," Arny looked around. He had the audience he was looking for.

"Question?"

"I take it you and Jenelle are really close."

"After going around for almost two years, I would hope so."

"Then the incident that brought the two of you together would be good thing, not something that would infuriate you."

After a bewildered agreement from Calvin, Arny continued, "Remember the last course-turn-around dance? I stole your date."

"The one when I thought Michelle was going to be my date?"

"Yeah. I was too late asking Michelle to go out with me. You had asked her first. I told her I was brokenhearted."

Chuckles broke out. Everyone knew Arny would never have to rely on a "broken heart" angle. It was rare that a girl ever turned him down.

"I got her to change her mind by telling her she was your third choice. That did it. She changed her mind and went with me."

Calvin said nothing.

Still partially squatting, Arny asked, "Since my dirty trick backfired and you ended up with the girl of your dreams, can you forgive me?"

"Had I known that before–"

"Yeah. I know. You'd have knocked my block off."

Calvin ignored Arny's injured foot and pushed him back on his butt. With a chuckle, he added, "You turkey. Michelle was so angry with me that she told me why she changed her mind. I let that guilt ride you." He returned to the extension ladder and signaled the boys to lower him.

Larry turned and whispered to Len, "What happened with Michelle?"

Len said, "She dumped them both."

The descent was farther than Calvin expected. Finally, he saw inside the five-foot high hole in the wall. The first disturbing sign his light revealed was water rushing down a trench about two feet deep. While the trench was barely half-full, there was no indication what rocks might lie in wait to twist a foot. He guessed the height of the bank on the left side of the one-foot wide trench to be about five feet. Walkable if you bent over, but as a landing spot, it would be a challenge. A landing area on the other side of the bank was almost negligible. Looking to the back of the hole, he saw a black surface, much like what was on the surface wall.

Only a cave? Can't be. Too much water pouring out to be a cave's mouth.

He tried inducing a swing to the rope. Through a pumping action, he redirected its motion. Before he finished aiming the rope to the hole, Graham called, "Hey. What are you doing?" Not wanting to explain his action from the end of a rope, Calvin asked to be brought up.

Once at the top, Calvin explained that he wanted to explore the hole to see if it was a cave or a tunnel. His plan was to be lowered a bit below the hole so he could step up into the landing. Coming from above meant dropping on to the landing, maybe slipping and falling or at least losing hold of the rope. "Don't want to be stranded there," he said. "At least not until we know if it is safe for us to all to go there."

Calvin's assumption that they would choose the opening as a means of escape gave way to a lively debate. Seeing no obvious conclusion, Larry closed the discussion.

"Let's help Calvin complete his search. Then we'll know if we have a decision to make."

IN THE END

Calvin's plan worked exactly as he had imagined. By slouching slightly, he stepped on to the dry landing at mouth of the hole. Immediately, he pointed the flashlight into heart of the darkness.

"Yes," said Calvin to himself. Looking up, he shouted, "I think it is a tunnel. Give me more rope."

Calvin proceeded an extra five feet and hooked his rope to a large piece of rock that had fallen from the ceiling. He tested the rope to make sure it was secure.

As he expected, the tunnel's interior matched the exterior, but what he hadn't thought of was that the tunnel would turn. It bent to the right after ten feet. The tunnel followed the running water for almost a hundred steps then branched away from the flowing water. Calvin's light poked a narrow path along the water flow, a path deep enough to crawl in and not drown. But could one find enough grip to climb the steep grade? The tunnel itself continued far beyond the range of his light, but it was enough to expose a pickax leaning against the wall. He wanted to continue investigating, but he knew his friends were anxiously awaiting his report. Exploration would have to wait. Returning to the mouth of the tunnel, he shouted the good news. He checked the bed of stream before it dumped its contents down the hole. The bottom was soft, muddy, and slippery.

CHAPTER 4

Tough Decision

C alvin's lengthy absence meant he had a lot of information to share when the boys pulled him back into the garage. However, not everyone was interested in what he had to say.

Worried that many of the boys were too excited about an exploration adventure, Jean raised his voice and interrupted efforts to get Calvin to spill his news. "Now, can talk about if we climb up to get out of here or go down?"

'Patience, patience," said Arny before Sampson could voice the same request. "Let's move to the other end of the garage where it's safe."

"And I want to hear what Calvin has to say first. Then we'll know if we even have a choice to make," said Sampson, nudging Brayden forward.

As Calvin followed the boys, he noticed a change. Two kerosene lanterns glowed at the far end of the garage. Sampson had found them in his father's camping gear.

"Okay, okay." Jean pushed his way to the front of the group, moving to the lanterns. He had no intention of being pushed to the back of the group where he might not be heard.

Several boys leaned against the workbench below the cupboard where the flashlights were. Some boys crowded at either end of the bench.

Standing before the boys, Sampson signaled Calvin to join him. When he arrived, Sampson said, "Tell us what you found."

Calvin gave a chronological report of his discoveries, excluding interpretations he had made. He wanted to see their honest reactions. Len and Arny didn't disappoint him. Their, "this could be fun," seconded his feelings. Sampson's practical, "we can't stay here," was what he expected. Then Jean jumped in.

"Of course, we can stay here. Who knows where Calvin's tunnel leads? It could come to a dead end. Then what will we do? There could be a maze of tunnels in there. We could get lost, be separated from each other. And that water flow. It could get steeper or even narrower. We leave here and any rescue efforts that come will never be able to find us. I say we stay where we are or look at how we might climb up out of here."

"You're right, Jean," began Arny. "But I for one am not looking forward to trying to climb out of here. One fall is enough for me." He rubbed his right hip, the part of his body that absorbed the initial shock of his fall. "Going down is a lot easier, and I'm looking forward to exploring the tunnel below, seeing where it goes. That's better than just sitting around here and doing nothing."

"You're just looking for an adventure." Jean stepped toward Arny. "What makes you think these tunnels are going to lead us anywhere worthwhile?"

"Because they were made by human beings."

Calvin's revelation grabbed everyone's attention.

"I didn't want to say anything because I was afraid that you'd think I was crazy. I first noticed a difference in the sides of the trench compared to the larger tunnel. They were smooth, worn away. I didn't think much of it even though the large tunnel looked like some amateur was hacking away at it. Then, farther in the tunnel, I saw a pickax standing against the wall."

"So?" said Brayden.

"So, someone made that tunnel." Calvin's brow wrinkled in surprise. *What's the matter with him? He should be able to figure that out.*

"And if someone made the tunnel, and we follow it, we'll find those people and be—"

"Rescued." Sampson finished Graham's statement at the same time that he did.

"Okay! Now you've really got my attention. I'm all for investigating this mystery." Len stepped up beside Calvin. "Who else is with us?" Arny and Samson left the bench and joined Calvin.

"Sampson, you an adventure seeker too?"

Looking at Victor, Sampson shook his head. "No. I just think that this building isn't going to stay wedged here for long. With the water eating away at the sides, it's just a matter of time before the rocks give way. I'd rather have my feet on solid ground."

"Makes sense." Victor glanced at Larry and Graham hoping to see a similar acceptance.

"And if you're worried you might miss a rescue effort, you could always leave a large note on this bench." Sampson knocked on it twice. "The note can explain where we can be found. Frankly, I don't think the garage will be here by the time rescuers show up."

"You really think so." Perry's voice was low. Almost as if he didn't want anyone else to hear him. Worried that someone might hear fear in his voice, Perry glanced to his side. Seeing no one close, he sidestepped away from the rest of the boys.

While Perry was talking, Terry joined Calvin's group.

"I do." Sampson's answer came back fast and confident.

"I doubt I can do what Calvin did. How else will I get down there?" Perry looked to Victor.

"Not a problem." Calvin had been planning for just such a question. "I'll go back down, and then whoever follows me—"

"Me," blurted Len.

"Will hold the rope tight. All you have to do is wrap one foot around the rope and slowly slide down. You know, slide down hand over hand so you can control your descent. When you get close, Len or I will grab and guide you onto the ledge. No trouble."

"You sure?" Perry still sounded uncertain.

"Absolutely."

"That's what I'm counting on," said Arny. "If I can make it with only one good foot, you'll have no trouble."

"Sounds like we'll have no trouble going down there to find Calvin's mystery men," said Len with a laugh.

"Your method sounds workable. I think I can handle it." Victor started to cross to Calvin's side, stopped, and walked up to Perry. His reassuring presence convinced Perry to come to Calvin's group.

"Brayden." Sampson caught him looking down, not wanting anyone to see the fear in his eyes. Brayden couldn't admit he is afraid he'd lose his grip on the rope and fall into the water below. Calvin's description made him think he might be able to do it.

"Brayden." Sampson's second call and his step toward Brayden forced Brayden to look up. "You really don't want to take a chance on this building crashing down. Not being able to swim means you won't make it."

"I know." His answer was quieter than Perry's voice.

"Then you're with us?"

Brayden nodded and walked to Sampson.

Larry looked at Jean. They were the only two left standing by the bench. "What's really bothering you?" he asked in a low voice.

Jean faced him and said, "I don't like rushed decisions. Even before we brought Calvin up, it sounded like the decision to go down was already made."

"Well, we can agree that each person does what they want, but do you really want to end up being here all alone? I will cross to Calvin's side. I think it's safer." Larry pointed to the rest of the group.

"Whatever." His answer was only loud enough for Larry to hear.

"I really would like you to join us."

Jean said nothing.

"I think the rest of the guys would too."

When Larry beckoned for Jean to come, Jean let Larry escort him to Calvin's side.

"Hope I don't regret this," Jean mumbled.

CHAPTER 5

What Is This Place?

Sampson hadn't planned on leading. His role started with the no-brainer idea that they bring the leftover food from their party. Calvin eagerly volunteered to pack them. He had to endure the boys complaining he'd dip into the snacks. When Sampson suggested that they also bring the two lanterns and spare kerosene can, Len acted on his suggestion. Jean reinforced Sampson's role as director by asking if they should take some of Sampson's father's camping gear. Sampson picked through his father's supplies. He added whatever he thought appropriate for a camping adventure. That included asking each boy to take a plastic grocery bag of potatoes.

"Oh boy. Fries for supper!" Len joked. "Don't forget the salt and ketchup."

Using a carpenter's pencil that he found on the bench, Jean scribbled a note on three labels used for identifying the length of nails in various cans:

"Escaped," "In tunnel," "In sinkhole." He stuck them on the cupboard door.

Their scavenging made a small dent in Mr. Sanfield's supply of potatoes, which he kept in an insulated storage bin at the front of the garage.

Perry aided Sampson during the whole evacuation procedure. Before leaving, he helped Sampson do a final review of what else could be taken from the garage. While Sampson appreciated Perry's assistance, he suspected Perry's true motivation. His suspicion grew stronger when he saw a small pile of the boys' jackets piled on a chair near the garage's front door. A small smile flashed across Perry's face.

Packing the jackets. One more delay, thought Sampson. *He's really afraid.*

As they stuffed the jackets into a plastic garbage bag, Sampson offered to take the jackets down. Perry took the camping rope that his father used to secure the tarp when they went camping. The rope and the bag of potatoes would be easy for Perry to handle and would serve as a suitable distraction while he worked his way down the rope.

Sampson grabbed the rope. When he saw Perry not stepping up with him, he asked, "Coming?"

Perry nodded. He approached Sampson and took the rope that Sampson handed to him. As soon as Sampson saw Perry pulled into the tunnel, he followed.

***

KEN SAIK

"Okay. We're done? Right?" Len looked to Sampson after he placed two bedrolls on the floor near the tunnel wall. Sampson nodded.

"Now we can look for Calvin's mysterious men?" Len looked to the other boys hoping for support. Many nodded. Holding a flashlight, Larry stepped up beside Len. Arny followed limping. Sampson looked at the forming search party.

"Go ahead," said Sampson. He watched Larry head down the dark passageway. It took only a few minutes for the pickax to appear and for them to quicken their pace. Sampson took a mental snapshot of the supplies that the boys lined up against the tunnel-wall entrance then he and Perry hurried after their friends.

By the time they caught up with the rest of the boys, Calvin had completed one swing of the pickax into the wall. His target was a football-sized rock. Chunks of clay and pebble-size stones fell. Calvin's second swing exposed half the rock.

"This is easy."

His third swing bounced off the side of rock and sent sparks flying. The pickax handle vibrated, causing Calvin to drop the tool. Len grabbed the ax. And with two more swings, he exposed so much of the rock that he could pry it free from the wall's hold.

"Stay here and play with your new toy if you want. I want to see what's farther down the tunnel." With that announcement, Larry and the boys proceeded. They stooped down to prevent their heads from hitting the ceiling.

60

Again, Sampson stayed behind and examined the scene. The cavity created by Len's effort matched pockmarks on both sides of the wall. It seemed like digging boulders from the wall was what the previous tunnel miners had been doing.

But why? What were they after?

No good reason was evident. Loose debris from Len's digging differed from the rest of the floor's contents. He guessed weathering and time had caused everything on the floor to be packed down. Looking at Perry, he said, "Guess we better get going."

Perry didn't move. Instead, he looked back into the tunnel they'd just come from.

"Something wrong?" asked Sampson, shining the light in the direction that Perry was looking.

"Do you get the feeling that we're being watched?"

"No," answered Sampson confidently.

"Sorry. Guess I'm feeling paranoid. All this darkness is playing tricks on me." Perry turned his back on his suspicions and walked to Sampson.

They caught up with the rest of the boys in time to catch a debate. Which way do they go? Three choices presented themselves. Calvin's choice—the path straight ahead, the one he could stand straight up in. It was not only higher but also wider.

Probably the previous miners' main passageway, thought Sampson. He glanced to the right to see a much smaller hole—lower, narrower. The same was the case for the one to his left except it seemed to be sharply angling up and heading back in the direction from which they came. Larry favored the latter passage saying it might lead back to the sinkhole but come out higher than the garage. Brayden argued for the one to the right. He and Jean dismissed the incline and the hope of getting to the surface.

"If I'm right," persisted Larry, "and we come out above the garage, we can still examine the possibility of climbing up to get out of here."

"I think we should concentrate on the main tunnel, the ones that the people before us put so much energy into enlarging," said Calvin. "I expect that it actually goes somewhere. Why else would they have put so much work into enlarging it?" He made a wild grab for Larry's flashlight, but Larry easily avoided his arm.

"Guys." Victor's voice rose over the others. Unlike his friends, Victor waited for everyone to stop talking. Brayden and Sampson silenced their friends standing near them.

"I think in a way Calvin's right. He's standing in what may be the main tunnel. For that reason, we should check the two side tunnels."

"What!" Calvin's remark temporarily turned faces to him, some shushing him.

"These smaller side tunnels probably won't go very far. Once we know that, we can confidently ignore them."

"Good idea," said Sampson. "Brayden and I and whoever else wants to, will explore the right tunnel. Larry, you and some of the guys check what's in the left side. Let's say we meet back here in half an hour. Sooner if we find a dead end just a little ways in."

Enjoying a clear direction for action, Larry invited Terry, Len, and Calvin to join him. Without waiting for an answer, he started off. Calvin shrugged and joined Len who was already hurrying into the tunnel. Some of the others followed.

In a half-squat Brayden, Jean, and Sampson probed the right tunnel's interior. It wiggled left, then right, as if the passage was created by the ground that offered the least resistance to being hollowed. The sharp turns limited the distance that they could see ahead. In order not to lose sight of each other, the boys placed a hand on the backs of the person in front of them. While the passageway widened a bit, the boys' feet frequently bumped into piles of boulders usually about six-foot long. Progress was slow. After a while, their backs demanded relief. Several times, Brayden called for Sampson so slow down so he could catch up.

In the other tunnel, progress was equally slow. Terry's "only five more minutes" figure of speech phrase met with "you have a watch?" There was no cell phone reception.

"Alright. Just another—" He paused to determine a reasonable number. "Fifty steps." Curiosity kept them struggling on.

Then Larry's "Dead end. Nothing here," ended their exploration. Larry passed the flashlight back to Graham who led the way back.

"What a waste of time," grumbled Calvin.

No one said anything. When the boys escaped the confines of their torturous tunnel, they stood in the main tunnel stretching and rubbing their backs. Calvin reclaimed the light from Graham. Standing in Terry's lantern-light, the boys talked. Calvin scouted ahead in the main tunnel. None of them noticed him disappear around the bend. His absence was only ten minutes, but his return coincided with the arrival of Brayden's team.

Brayden's report, "nothing special," dismissed several facts that distinguished their route from Larry's. While Brayden's passageway twisted right and left and up and down, sometimes sharply, they frequently were able to stand straight up. Time didn't permit them to explore to the end of their tunnel. Sampson noted one other difference in their reports. While his group encountered rocks piled on the floor, Larry's group found none. When he mentioned that fact, no one ventured an explanation for the difference.

The moment Calvin thought there was a break in the conversation, he caught the attention of Arny and Len. "Let's move on." With a quick tilt of his head in the direction of the unexplored tunnel, he turned and led the way.

"Yeah. Let's find out what's at the end of Calvin's tunnel." Larry hurried after his friends.

Occasionally, the boys encountered a branch tunnel. The first time that happened, Calvin said that they could explore the branch tunnels later, if they had time. His steady strolling pace left no time to debate or to wander away.

For every tunnel Sampson passed, he shot a quick beam of light down each passage. He noted sometimes these diversions departed at a sharp angle. Other times they veered right or left but still in the same general direction they'd been walking. Every now and then a tunnel path headed back in the direction from which they came. The narrower, shorter tunnels made it easier for him to bypass.

In a low squeaky kid's voice, Arny uttered, "Are we there yet?"

Calvin, who was fifteen paces ahead heard his friend. He stopped and turned to find a grinning face. "Foot bothering you?"

Arny lied. "No. But we've been walking for hours." Limping, he drew closer to Calvin.

Jean pulled Calvin's hand, so the light shone on his wristwatch. "Actually, it's only been about twenty-five minutes."

Jean wore a multifunctioning wristwatch in reaction to his friend's dependence on their cells. It was a test to see if they would still accept him for who he was. Terry was the only other boy who wore a wristwatch, a gift from his uncle, to him a very special man. He also carried a cell.

In spite of Arny's answer, Calvin took a five-minute breather. He watched his friend massage his ankle. When Calvin started again, he set a slower pace. The next time he stopped, he faced a fork, two tunnels, each of the same height and same width.

Anticipating Calvin's question, Len said, "Let's split up. You," he said, pointing to Calvin take the high road." He paused to see how closely his friend was following him, "Or left road if you like. And you guys"— he pointed to Brayden, Perry, and Sampson— "take the other road. An hour tops. When you return, then we'll decide which way we'll go. I'm staying behind with Arny." He gently slapped Arny's back.

The moment Arny opened his mouth to object, Len drowned him out, "Cut the macho bull. Be smart and say thanks. That foot of yours needs a rest whether you believe it or not. If you were a player on my soccer team, I'd have benched you for the rest of the game." The boys accepted Len's directions. Each team chose someone with a watch. That way they could explore for half an hour before returning.

While their friends were exploring, to help pass the time, Arny and Len began playing rock, paper, scissors. In the lantern light, Arny found himself being distracted by the lantern's dancing flame and the shaking shadows. On average, for every four turns they played, Arny won once. After five minutes, he quit.

Instead of the game, they speculated about whether the rain quit, whether their parents were out with the first responders looking for them, whether anyone saw their rope hanging from the garage door beam. They leaned against the wall and closed their eyes. They agreed that when they returned for the supplies, they would check to see if there was any sign that people were searching for them.

CHAPTER 6

NEWS

Conrad, Terry, and Graham returned first.

"Sleeping!" said Graham the moment his flashlight spotlighted the two boys.

"Doctor's orders," explained Arny, pointing to Len. He chuckled.

"Arny said he couldn't sleep, so I had to model it for him." Len delivered his defense with no hesitation.

"Dirty job," said Graham, smiling.

"Exactly. Why you back so soon?" Len stood up and helped Arny to his feet

"We found a huge cavern. Looks like it was a home for someone." He looked to Terry, who nodded to second Graham's description.

"Calvin's mystery men?" asked Arny with a smile.

"Seriously, yes. There's camping equipment, like a Coleman stove, two lanterns, a lot of personal stuff, and—"

"But no sign of people?" asked Len.

"Right. And from the looks of things, no one's been around for some time."

"You know this because?" Len stretched.

"Dust caked on everything. And get this. Three other passages lead out of the cavern, all heavily used. At least that's what we think given the size of the tunnels.

"So, are the other guys exploring those other tunnels?"

"No. Thanks to Brayden and his lighter—he lit the mystery men's lanterns. That provided the rest of the guys with the light they needed to start checking the cavern out. Last I saw they were examining the personal articles lying around. I think they're waiting until we return. Exploring tunnels is better done with flashlights. They cast a light farther."

"So, what do we do now?" asked Arny.

"Look! There's another one." Graham's interruption redirected their attention. He aimed his beam to the wall over the tunnel from where their supplies were stored. Several small rocks formed a circle. A line of rocks ran through the middle. "I saw that same sign over all the branch tunnels as I worked my way back here."

"Don't enter," interpreted Len.

"Or danger," added Arny.

"Well we know what's down that way," said Len, pointing to the tunnel that Graham indicated. "Nothing. Do not enter could mean the passage goes nowhere important."

"Maybe I should go back and check out a couple of the other tunnels. See if that's the case," said Graham, pointing his light down the tunnel that lead to the cavern.

Len seconded Graham's suggestion. He didn't want Arny to do any more walking than was necessary. Not wanting to admit his foot bothered him, Arny challenged Graham's proposal. He said they should remain together until Sampson and the others returned. Finding out what the symbol meant could be done later. Before they could come to a decision, Sampson and the rest of the boys appeared.

Sampson reported. A passageway kept on going up, only two stubby branch-tunnels that ended with wide piles of rocks.

They agreed to investigate the cavern Graham found. Graham took the lead, setting a slow pace. "For Arny's benefit," he said. He wanted to shine his light down the "do not enter" passages. Sampson also took a quick look down each passage.

As they went back to the cavern, Graham said, "Hey! Look at this." Without waiting for the others to catch up, he half-squatted and headed into the opening on his right. The boys crowded around the entrance and saw Graham's light focused on a reddish boulder half the size of a quad. Light flashed in many directions from hundreds of gold speckles embedded in the rock. At first glance, it seemed the tunnel ended six feet in, but as Graham neared the obstruction, he veered to the right. Someone had dug around the rock.

"Unbelievable." Graham brushed some loose gravel from the top. To the boys it appeared the intent was to roll it out to the main tunnel. The boys agreed that rolling out of the tunnel was an impossible task. Their discussion told Graham to forget about his find and return to leading them to the cavern. Two more openings appeared before they arrived at their destination. Each time, he directed a beam of light at a circle of stones near the entrance of the tunnels.

Graham found Larry, Jean, and Calvin. They were sitting on small boulders in a semicircle. Three seats opposite them remained available. One lantern sat in the middle on a tall thin rock. The other sat in a hollowed-out ledge in the wall between two exits.

The moment Calvin saw Arny limp into their presence he stood up and directed his friend to his seat. "Sit here. I warmed it up for you."

Laughing, Larry said, "A-h-h come on now. You're not going to start babying him, are you?"

"Like he's my brother." Calvin grinned, expecting to see a frown on Arny's face. There was none. "Come on, bro," said Calvin, reaching out. Arny accepted Calvin's help without objection. After Arny passed by him, Calvin's smile disappeared. He imagined Arny's pain.

Larry told the late arrivals that he and Calvin had lettered the exits from the cavity in which they stood. From left to right they were A, B, C, and D. The last one was from where their supplies were. About fifteen feet farther down tunnels B and C a semicircular connecting tunnel joined tunnels B and C. Off the connecting tunnel were two more storage areas. In a wide section of the semicircular tunnel, Larry found a countertop. Calvin's mystery men had placed two large flat rocks on a two-foot long clay base. Scattered on the counter were some gray ceramic bowls, metal cutlery, large pots and pans. Shoved in the back of a hole in the wall that served as a shelf, he also found some small capped storage bins.

A short distance down passageway A, Calvin showed them two large rooms. They were close to the cavern or what Calvin called "Home Base." By the size of these rooms, Calvin guessed a large number of men had worked here. He presumed the rooms served either as sleeping quarters, storage areas, or both. Each room had a lantern. There was no end in sight for tunnel A either.

Tunnels B and D had the *no entry* symbol over them, but tunnels A and C didn't. Larry was surprised to hear that Graham observed the *no entry* symbols over almost all the side tunnels in the D passageway.

Calvin suggested that they make Home Base, their headquarters. Unlike the area where they left their supplies, this place was spacious and dry. When no one objected, Larry began listing the tools that they found in the storage section near the B tunnel—shovels, pickaxs, two broad metal-wheeled square carts.

"Sampson." Urgency marked Calvin's call. He was seated looking at Arny's swollen foot. "Got a first aid kit in the supplies we brought down?"

Sampson nodded. "Yes."

"Are there tensor bandages in there?"

Sampson nodded again.

"Can someone bring the kit down here?" asked Calvin.

"Glad to," Sampson volunteered. "And we'll bring the supplies here at the same time."

Len and Perry offered to help. On their way back, Len wondered how any potential rescuers would know how to find them.

At their supply depot, Len looked up to the garage to see if there was any sign of their parents or first responders. He saw none. He frowned. "We have to leave something here in case rescuers come. Then they will know this is where we ended up."

His friends stopped picking up their gear, but no one said anything.

"Do we have some paper and a pen? Len asked, looking around. "I could sketch a map showing where we moved to."

"Check the brown canvas duffel bag," said Sampson.

While Len searched for the steno pad and black felt pen, Sampson told him to look out for a plastic bag with safety pins. "You can use it to pin your map to a jacket, one we'll leave here." Thinking that two jackets would be more easily seen, Sampson volunteered to leave his jacket behind. Len did too.

As they walked back to their headquarters, Len counted the steps from their supplies to the cavern. Halfway there, he lost track.

Sampson told him they would have to take three more trips to bring the rest of their things. "Do your count on the next return trip." Len settled for remembering the number of branch passageways on either side of their path. When he reached home base, he noted their trip included three tunnels branching to the right and five to the left. While Calvin bandaged Arny's foot, Len sketched a map. He included the headquarters with its four entrances.

Sampson looked at Len's map. "Good enough. Does the job," he said and walked over to check on Arny.

"Kind of simple," said Graham after glancing at Len's work.

Brayden looked over Len's shoulder at the map and agreed. Len shot him an angry look.

"It lacks detail. You know, how many steps from each branch tunnel." Brayden shook his head.

"You think you're so smart, you do it then." Len threw the steno pad. It missed Brayden and fell to the ground.

"Guys. For potential rescuers, it may do the job. And it's better than nothing. Thanks, Len." Sampson walked up to Brayden. He raised a hand and stopped him from challenging Len again. "Although Brayden does have a point. We may be stuck here for some time."

"Pessimist," said Calvin.

"It might be helpful if we have our own map showing what we've discovered. I know there are too many tunnels to keep in my head." Sampson looked around at his friends. No put downs. In a lower tone, he asked, "Anyone like to take on that job?"

"Waste of time," mumbled Jean.

"Be easier than crawling around in some of these small tunnels." Sampson looked to Arny hoping he'd step up.

"Okay. I'll try." Perry went over, picked up the pad, and took the pen from Len. He tore out the page with Len's work and gave it to him.

With the exception of Arny and Calvin, the other boys went with Sampson to bring the rest of the supplies. Perry carried a lantern so he could make notes of the number of steps between each side passageway. He saw all of them had the small circle of stones near the entrance except for the passage at the fork that he and Sampson had explored. It was also the only one that went up. He showed the pathway as open because they never came to its end.

As soon as they reached their supplies, Perry started making a good copy of his map. He took time to include all the details he had seen. Because all the boys came, they were able to take all the supplies back on their first trip.

As the boys began to head back to Home Base, Perry said, "Anybody staying back with me?"

Larry, who was one of the last to leave, turned and said, "Don't be a wimp." He looked at Perry, but Perry turned his attention to his map and said nothing. He left when he completed his map. On the way back to the cavern, he checked the accuracy of his work.

IN THE END

When Perry returned to Home Base, he noticed sleeping bags stretched out. Some boys were sleeping. A couple boys raised their heads for a moment and waved to Perry. Two lanterns were turned very low. Sampson pointed to an empty sleeping bag near him. Perry accepted the suggestion without hesitation. They'd been up for almost twenty hours.

The boys awoke to a feather-brush breeze. If it wasn't for the ground-hard bed, the boys could have taken another hour or two of shut-eye.

Terry checked his watch. It was after eight. "Morning, so soon," he mumbled.

Sampson got up and started the morning activities by going to the cooking area to make breakfast. Between his supplies and what the mystery men left, Sampson was able to make pancakes. Len and Larry entered to offer some help. Larry quipped, "What! No sausages?"

And from Len, "No syrup? Boy, this will be the last time we're coming over to your place for breakfast."

Sampson directed them to boil water for tea. Good news. He had sugar. No coffee. Sampson's pancakes received thanks from the rest of the boys. He had liberally sprinkled them with cinnamon. "Like slices of toast without jam," Len teased. After breakfast, Sampson found some peanut butter in his supplies. *I'll put that on the pancakes next time.*

While Brayden and Conrad cleaned up, Calvin gathered the guys together. An inviting morning breeze flowed from the C tunnel and disappeared down passages A and D. Calvin recommended that they explore passageway C.

All the boys readily agreed with Calvin except Arny. He wanted to rest his swollen foot. He volunteered to read through one of the journals left by the mystery men. Perry said he'd stay behind and work on his maps and keep Arny company. Jean recommended that some of them explore passage B to see why there was a no entry symbol over it. He received no support.

With cleanup completed, all ten boys began their trek. The breeze increased. After a long walk, Sampson turned off his flashlight. They picked their way along the rough path. Graham speculated that a continual strong breeze could have swept away any loose sand or clay particles thus exposing the bare rocks that they had to step over carefully.

The first new opening they found was on their left. Inside that tunnel and onward in the C tunnel a three-foot-wide cobble stone pathway made walking easier. Jean asked Sampson for the flashlight so he could explore the branch tunnel's cobblestone path. Sampson agreed. No one accompanied Jean, but that didn't bother him.

As the boys continued down the tunnel C path, scratch-mark scars on the pathway caught Sampson's attention. He assumed they had been made by one of the two broad metal-wheeled square carts at Home Base. After a five-minute walk, the boys came upon another tunnel branching off to the right. The cobblestone path entered the tunnel and stopped after two feet. The balance of the flooring was marked with indented cartwheel scars.

"Anyone for exploring this tunnel?" asked Calvin. Larry and Len responded. Len turned on his flashlight and started down the branch tunnel.

For the rest of the boys, progress grew faster. No protruding rocks or potholes impeded their exploration. Daylight appeared ahead. The boys quickened their pace. After a hundred steps, a long thirty-foot deep crevice created by an earthquake several decades ago halted their advance. Across the divide, a path continued. No cobblestones there. A short distance away, a high waterfall splashed into a small lake. The beauty of the blue sky held most of the boy's attention.

"Not even a cloud," murmured Brayden.

Calvin was overwhelmed with joy for a different reason.

Cold water I'll bet! Just what Arny needs for his foot!

"Wow! That's steep!" said Calvin, shaking his head looking down the crevice.

What a depth! Straight down. Nothing to slow the descent. Boulder landing. Not good. Looking to the opposite side of the crevice, Calvin saw the same challenge. *Gotta find a way across.*

Off to his right side, a narrow stone ledge offered hope. A little farther, the crevice wall cut into the side of the rock face. Calvin couldn't see around it. Even farther out where the crevice ended, another ledge appeared. *A possible way around this drop.* He stepped to the side of the path and tested the strength of the ledge with one foot. No sign of giving under his weight.

"What do you think you're doing?" challenged Conrad. He moved closer to Calvin in preparation to pull him away from edge.

"I've gotta find a way to that water." He pointed to the waterfall. "Arny's foot really needs a cold compress. That will do it."

"Won't do him any good if you fall." Conrad looked around for help. A quick wave of his hand prompted Sampson's support.

"He's right, Calvin. Wait and see if the rope we brought will reach the bottom. You could easily rappel down."

"And what about going back up on the other side? Who will be there to hold the rope assuming it is long enough?" When Calvin saw his objection stumped his objectors, he added, "I just want to go to the bend in the ledge. See if the ledge continues and will support a person."

"You feel any movement under your feet you step back here immediately. Understand? Falling's not an option." Sampson followed his instruction by taking a step closer to Calvin. It put him within an arm's reach from his friend.

"Don't worry. I couldn't agree with you more." He turned his red cap around so the visor wouldn't rub against the wall and fall off.

With his stomach pressed firmly against the face of the rock, Calvin extended his right foot. Almost no weight on the toe. His toe brushed the side of the rock. Success. Nothing loose. He transferred the rest of his weight to his right foot. No problem detected. He slid his left foot up to the right foot. In that fashion, he inched along the ledge, one foot, then a second, and then a third foot. As he neared the ledge's bend four and a half feet away from his starting point, he leaned forward to peak around the side to see how far the ledge extended.

For a second or two, he stared in disbelief. The width of the ledge narrowed to an inch, sometimes two. He considered using his foot to carve a wider base. His hope ended with a slight movement under his right foot.

Step back.

He jerked it back. The instinctive reaction resulted in his left foot sliding away from the right. He forgot about keeping his left toe tight against the rock face. The support beneath his left foot began to give under his weight.

No choice.

Calvin's right foot pressed harder and propelled his body up in a leftward direction. The attempted jump failed. Support beneath both his feet gave way. The front of Calvin's feet slid against the clay rock face. One foot struck a firmly wedged rock and projected Calvin into a dive. His red cap flew off. Calvin's "no", was the only scream that emerged before he hit something solid. On the way down, his head struck a rock. A split second of pain. A floating sensation and a vague image of his body about to be pasted to the rocks below. Dizziness, then nothing.

Sampson and Conrad's, "Calvin. Calvin." did nothing to break his fall. When Calvin hit the bottom of the crevice, all the boys stood in silence hoping to see some sign of movement.

Impossible.

Can't be.

Oh my god. It can't be.

Please, dear God, don't take him from us.

Unreal.

Brayden's call, "Calvin. Calvin," brought no response. Spurred by Brayden's desperate call, Len and Larry ran up to the boys.

"What happened?" they said in unison.

***

In the meantime, at Home Base, Perry held out his tunnel maps for Arny to examine. Proudly, he pointed to the labels. One letter for each of the four main cavern passages, (A, B, C, D). Each branch tunnel received an uppercase letter to signify the starting point of a tunnel from Home Base. The same letter in lowercase indicated the end of the tunnel. Dead tunnels had no letter. Each tunnel was also numbered from Home Base. The tunnel's designation corresponded to a detailed drawing of the tunnel on a separate page. It illustrated branch tunnels that had additional limbs.

IN THE END

While Perry had been designing his maps, Arny had been reading what he understood to be a report or a journal of one of Calvin's mystery men. The information described progress in various tunnels, some of which Arny could see on Perry's map. Accidents were frequent. Men died. One report recorded a massive cave-in in the passage that led back to their home. Many men died. Arny guessed that was tunnel B.

After the cave-in, their efforts switched from mining to finding a route back to their home, a place they called Vanna. They discovered they mistakenly explored the same tunnels several times. Then *no entry* symbols—a circle of rocks with a bar through it—were imbedded in the walls.

Hope of getting home was raised when they found a tunnel that opened up to daylight. A deep fissure blocked their way. By pouring rocks and boulders into the fissure they hoped to work their way to the other side and fresh water. Progress was slow, back breaking. Eventually, they quit in favor of going down the dark tunnels again. Tunnel A, Arny guessed. That option meant poking through maze after maze. Men complained but it demanded less effort than climbing steep rock faces like mountain goats. The group decided to dedicate all their efforts into that option to get home. Many tunnels led nowhere. Then the reports stopped.

The Vanna descriptions impressed Arny. He was about to tell Perry about Vanna when they heard footsteps coming from tunnel C. Turning, they first saw a flashlight beam. Sampson appeared with his head down looking at a red cap that he held in his hands. Len and Larry appeared next carrying Calvin's body.

Arny and Perry hurried to Sampson. Sampson reported on the accident. His description included the forbidding depth of the fissure and the waterfall that Calvin attempt to reach.

As Arny listened, he shuffled to Calvin's body, picked up his friend's hand, and then wiped his tears away. The rest of the boys clustered around Perry and Arny, some laying their hand on Arny.

"If the crevice was so deep, how did you get Calvin's body out?" asked Perry.

Larry responded by telling of the downward sloping tunnel that they had explored. Not only did it cut the drop by almost a half, but the mystery men had been pouring sand and clay down the side. It made sliding to the bottom possible. From there, Len and Larry picked up Calvin's body. After climbing up a way, they were able to lift it up to Graham and Sampson. They hoisted the body farther up the slope to Victor and Brayden.

"What are we going to do with him?" asked Conrad looking to Victor.

"Bury him, of course," answered Arny, not looking up from the body. His sharp voice dared anyone to contest his response. He didn't move. Sampson put a gentle guiding hand on Arny's shoulder, gave him Calvin's red cap, and nudged him toward Home Base.

IN THE END

"Where's the best place?"

Brayden's question met with silence. Whispering to Terry, Conrad suggested near the pit where they had originally placed their supplies. Terry agreed suggesting that if rescuers came, they would find Calvin's body quickly.

Turning to face Terry and Conrad, Sampson said, "Suggestion?"

Conrad nudged Terry to speak. He didn't want to risk irritating Arny again. In response to Sampson's question, Arny said in a less emotional tone, "I'd like to see him placed close to us, maybe in one of those rooms off Tunnel A."

Victor and Brayden volunteered to dig a shallow grave. The rest of the boys sat around Calvin's body telling stories about their friend. When Jean arrived, they explained what had happened. He stayed with the group for a while sharing a couple of his Calvin stories, and then went to help Victor and Brayden.

Digging was slow. The first couple of inches of sand came off easily. Then they hit gravel and larger rocks, some of which needed to be pried loose. Brayden gratefully surrendered his pickax to Jean. While Jean dragged the larger rocks out of the hole, he told Brayden and Victor about his discoveries at the end of tunnel B.

Jean figured a cave-in had occurred there. He told them he had taken some of the large rocks from the cave-in and placed them in a nearby empty cart.

By removing the remaining loose gravel, he found a metal-wheeled cart filled only with large rocks.

Victor suggested it was being brought to fill the crevice. He'd seen a large pile of rocks at the bottom of the fissure. He guessed the men were trying to fill that section of the crevice. On the bottom of the opposite side of the crevice, he saw a flat surface. He speculated they were building a raised platform so that they could reach the top of the fissure. The height of the rebuilt platform suggested the men had been laboring for some time.

Terry and Conrad came to check on Brayden and Victor's progress. The hole had become a six-foot trench nestled against the entrance wall of the first large room from Home Base. It was wide enough for a body but not quite a foot deep.

In response to Terry's comment about the shallowness of the hole, Jean asked, "Wanna help?" He stepped out of the trench and handed the pickax to Terry.

"Maybe the hole's deep enough. If it isn't, we can always stack the rocks and sand you dug to cover Calvin's body." The moment Terry uttered those words, he stopped. He looked at Victor. His face wore a similar shocked expression.

"You don't suppose—" Victor couldn't reveal what he had just realized.

"Suppose what?" asked Conrad who was only half following their conversation.

"Those piles of rocks we've been seeing in the branch tunnels, they're graves," explained Terry.

IN THE END

The boys stood in silence, one counting the number of possible grave sites, one feeling guilty for cursing the rocks that narrowed passages or stubbed toes.

Jean said in a low voice as if speaking to himself, "That's why tunnel B is lined with raised piles of rocks along one side. They're for buried bodies from the cave-in. So many people."

Brayden recommended that they accept Terry's suggestion, and they use the rocks that they had dug up to cover Calvin's body. The boys agreed. Terry and Conrad went back to tell the rest of their friends. Because they thought there wasn't enough material to cover Calvin's body, they went with Jean down tunnel B to help him push one of the metal-wheeled carts containing rocks.

Victor asked Perry if he would lead their memorial service. At the graveside, Perry asked that they repeat the Lord's Prayer first. He thanked God for the forgiveness of their sins so that at a time like this they could look in confidence to the future, to a time when they would all be together again. When they would be reunited in God's house. After they all shared some stories about Calvin, they placed his cap on the pile of rocks and returned to Home Base.

CHAPTER 7

What Now?

"Look out below."

Brayden's warning wasn't needed. Over the last several days, the boys committed themselves to watching out for each other more rigorously. Calvin's needless death weighed heavily.

Len and Larry stood at the bottom of the crevice and looked up. They waved to Brayden and backed away from the spill area. With a nod from Brayden, Graham pushed the cart to the edge of the fissure and dumped its half load of large rocks. Being the heaviest boys, they were the mules who pushed the heavy carts on the cobblestone path from tunnel B to the crevice.

Len and Larry waited at the bottom. They would pick through the rocks and choose the ones most useful for building stone steps at the top of the ramp. By wedging rocks in, Len and Larry, nicknamed stone masons, built two steps each rising almost a foot.

IN THE END

Using a small metal pail, Perry picked up the smaller rocks and spilled them along the ramp. The other boys in tunnel B dug through the caved-in gravel and placed the smaller rocks in one of the two metal carts.

Hard work lengthened the ramp and widened the base. The hope was to build along the fissure side to climb close to the top. Then they would have access to fresh water and be able to complete Calvin's goal of getting a cold-water compress for Arny's foot.

The tensor bandage helped, but the pain and the swelling remained. Arny felt frustrated by the forced inactivity. The other boys insisted that he stay off his feet.

When Len and Larry finished building the second one-foot square step up, Len questioned doing another one. The last step was unstable. Large stones were becoming scarce. No new grips appeared on the face of the crevice wall. If they constructed another foot, the greater extension might fall. Larry had let Len stand on his shoulders, but Len couldn't see any grips farther up the face of the wall.

If only I could say, guys, let's forget this, Len thought. He shook his head. So much work had been put into lengthening the ramp along the crevice wall. Perry had blisters on his hands from carrying the pail of gravel from the spill area to the ramp. Working in the hot sun meant drinking more water. Their supply was running low.

At first it made so much sense, thought Len. *That's what the mystery men had been doing.*

The mystery men's ramp had risen a person's height. Calvin had thought the boys could do that too. The guys agreed. However, when they saw how long it was taking to increase the ramp's height, the guys became discouraged. Len had admonished, "We can't let Calvin's death be for nothing." In a thought-less moment, he volunteered to be the new Spider-Man and climb the face of the fissure.

Then he suggested constructing stone steps to increase the height sooner. The first foot-high steps took little time. Not so with the last step.

Looking at height to the top, he said to Larry in a whisper, "I wish I could back out."

In a low voice, Larry said, "Do that and the guys will never take any of your ideas seriously."

As Len stood at the bottom of the crevice, he eyed the smooth-faced wall, the impossible task. No alternative strategies surfaced. Then someone walked up behind him.

"Not looking too good, is it?" Sampson asked.

"No," he said, turning to face his friend. Len noticed a pickax in Sampson's hand. *Does he expect me to hack out grips?* he wondered. *Might work for the first couple of feet, but not once I get higher. I wouldn't be able to swing that tool. Be too heavy.*

"I have an idea that might make your climb easier." Sampson raised both his hands, one with the pickax and the other with their last rope. He tied one end of the rope at the head of the pickax, and he made a tight loop near the other end. "I think we can use this as an anchor. We'll throw it up and hook it in the rocks above. By hanging onto the rope, you can climb up the face of this wall. What do you think?" Sampson whipped the rope out to show it was long enough to get to the top.

"Not what I had in mind, but it could work. Hope the rope's strong enough to hold me," Len said, "It's only half the diameter of the rope we used to be lowered down from the garage."

"Not to worry. Perry, Larry, and I will use a sleeping bag to make a net to catch you if it breaks, but I don't think we'll need it," said Sampson.

Perry joined Sampson and Len. Grinning, Larry added, "Hope you're not too heavy. I'd hate to drop you and have another gimpy guy in our group." He chuckled as he nudged Perry and shifted the sleeping bag to his other arm.

"Like to try?" asked Sampson. He glanced up and then handed the pickax tied with the rope to Len.

After four attempts, Len anchored the pickax. He gave the rope a gentle tug, then a harder one. He hung his weight on the rope. No movement. "Stand back," he said. He jumped up and grabbed the rope so that his fall jerked hard. The anchor held.

"Looks promising," said Len with a grin. He looked to his friends. "Spidy, ready for action." Leaning back, he placed his runners against the wall, took three steps up, and glanced back to see his sleeping bag net unfolding.

"Just in case," said Sampson.

Len turned his attention to his task. He leaned forward. His legs bent as he prepared to walk up the side of the wall.

"Hey," called Sampson. "Pull yourself up hand over hand. Otherwise, when you get to the top, the pickax may come off."

Len nodded and climbed up the face of the fissure as if he'd been doing it all his life. When he reached the top, he looked down and said, "Piece of cake." Pointing to Larry, he added, "You try."

Sampson stopped Larry as he moved into position. "Our purpose is to get a cold compress for Arny, remember?" He pulled a hand towel from his back pocket and gave it to Larry. Larry tucked it under his belt next to two water bottles.

Larry grabbed the rope and began his ascent. After going up several feet, he stopped, twisted one of his feet in the rope, tested to make sure there was no slipping and leaned away from the wall. He looked down at his friends to see if they were admiring his ability.

"Look, Mom, no net." He laughed and looked up to see if Len got the joke. He did. Larry continued his climb. At the top, he accepted Len's hand up.

They waved to Graham and Brayden who were standing by their empty cart on the other side of the crevice. Then they jogged halfway to the small lake, filled the water bottles, and soaked the hand towel and walked back to Sampson and Perry.

"Ready," called Larry as he prepared to drop the dripping hand towel to Sampson.

IN THE END

Before Sampson approached the side of the wall, Len took the towel from his friend. With an index finger to his lips and a huge grin, he silenced Larry's objection. He looked down and saw Sampson with his arms extended over his head to catch the towel. Leaning back, Len threw the towel hard straight at Sampson's head. Sampson's "jerk" sent Larry and Len bending over in laughter.

"Cold enough for you?" asked Len. His laughter erased the answer.

Sampson tossed the wet cloth up to the waiting Brayden who then left to see Arny. Graham had pushed the empty cart back to the tunnel where Jean and the others were filling the other two carts. Graham's news of their success brought Jean and his helpers to Home Base to see Arny.

Out of habit, Perry and Sampson each brought another pail of small rocks to the base of the platform while Len and Larry scaled down to them. All four boys returned to Home Base.

Arny was propped up against one boulder on a bedroll and another two to cushion his back. A folded bedroll was neatly spread beneath his raised foot, the foot with an ankle wrapped up in a damp hand towel.

Len's "coffee break time" started Perry and Sampson peeling potatoes. A pan was placed on the Coleman stove to fry the potato wedges. Perry grabbed the ketchup. The rest of the boys swallowed some of the water that Larry had brought back in his water bottle. Idle conversation turned to "What's next?"

"Finding a way out of here." Victor's response was greeted by agreement from Brayden, Perry, and Jean.

"Home," you mean," said Larry, looking to Len for confirmation.

Len nodded.

"Out of here, at least," added Jean.

"Out of here could mean finding this Vanna," said Arny. "While you guys have been working your buns off, I've been going through some of the journals. This guy wrote a lot about Vanna. It's like a holiday resort."

"So, tell us about it," said Jean. "What makes it such a great place?"

"From a fun perspective, it has basketball, squash, and tennis courts, Olympic-size swimming pools, and best of all, horseback riding stables with trails."

"No bikes?"

"Bikes and electric scooters seem to be the main form of transportation in the cities. It appears trucks only enter the city to carry food from family farms and goods from cottage farm enterprises. A rapid transit system serves an industrial area and another for a commercial area."

"You getting all that from this guy's journal?" asked Sampson.

"Yeah, the guy appears to be a wannabe reporter, a writer. He has short stories about interesting people living there. That's how I learned about the transit system. He's even written a few poems about Vanna. Next time I find a good one, I'll mark it and read it to you."

"Could it be that this guy is just a fiction writer?" asked Terry.

"What's the weather like? Or didn't you get a weather report?" asked Larry.

"From the stories, if one takes that as fact, it sounds very Caribbean. In other words, hot."

"I'm really starting to like that place," said Victor.

"Yeah," added Len. "How soon can we leave for Vanna?" Looking at Sampson, he added, "Not that I mean to complain, but I'm getting tired of Sampson's pancakes. Thanks for adding the new flavor to this morning's pancakes. Charcoal, wasn't it?"

Len looked to Larry for a nod of approval.

"I don't know about the rest of you, but I would like to go home," said Larry.

Facing Larry, Jean said, "Forget returning home. None of these tunnels lead to the surface. Unless we find a shaft going up, we're out of luck."

"Not impossible," objected Larry, looking to his friends for support. He saw no one nodding in agreement.

"Actually, it is impossible. While Len and Larry were making like mountain goats, I was looking up at the blue sky, thinking about where this opening might be on the surface. I saw no planes. It made me suspect that we are in some kind of a restricted area," said Victor.

"Like what?" asked Larry.

"Maybe the federal reserve outside of town."

"You mean that huge area with a ten-foot chain-link fence?" asked Sampson.

"And barbed wire strung along the top leaning out,'" added Len.

"And signs saying, 'Danger. Keep out," added Larry.

"I don't know what's so dangerous about that place. All I've seen is an overgrown forest and dead trees," said Len

"Whatever. I've never seen any planes over the area," said Graham.

"No roads leading into that wilderness area," said Sampson.

"All that means is that a rescue from above is not likely," said Jean. "We need to find a way out of these tunnels."

Jean's suggestion redirected their attention on which route they should use. There was no consensus. Some favored tunnel C and the daylight it offered. It showed signs of ascending. Maybe the surface was reachable.

"You want to make like worms and crawl around in the dark?" asked Conrad, referring to exploring tunnel A. Sampson pointed out that advancing into the depths of the rock formation would be easier than being a mountain goat. Jean favored continuing to hollow a gravel path through tunnel B, the mystery men's most direct route to Vanna. He argued that it was probably the mystery men's first priority. Why else would they have bothered to create such a wide tunnel and a cobble stone pathway for moving debris?

Agreement centered around giving Arny's foot one more day to heal. In the meantime, each of them would spend a little more time exploring their preferred option. Afterwards, they would meet again to see if they could come to an agreement.

Sampson worried there'd be no agreement. Each might choose to go their own way. In one-to-one conversations, he planted the idea that they stood a better chance of succeeding if they stuck together. They'd be better able to look out for each other.

Before breaking up to start their investigations, the boys agreed to meet for supper in another six hours. Victor had estimated that's when the sun would set. Victor, Len, Larry, and Conrad chose to explore the tunnel C option. Jean planned on going to tunnel's B caved-in area. Terry, Sampson, Perry, and Brayden intended to check out a part of tunnel A.

Arny sat with his leg up wrapped in the cold compress. Graham promised to stay back and empty the carts for Jean. That way he could make a few runs to the lake to wet towels for Arny's foot. Arny wasn't thrilled about reading more boring work-related journal reports. He hoped to find more stories or poems about Vanna, but in the last pages, they were less frequent.

Three and half hours later as Arny was reading, he heard a rumbling. Shortly, Graham came rushing out of tunnel C and into the headquarters. Arny pointed to tunnel B.

Graham charged off and soon encountered a cloud of dust. Sweeping actions by his hands to clear the air didn't help. To see better, he slowed down. He coughed. Then he came to a dead stop. Fresh gravel blocked his path. One of the two carts that Jean had filled was barely visible, but no Jean. He screamed his friend's name. Silence.

He stumbled up the graveled pile. Bowling-ball-sized rocks were frantically tossed aside. He clawed at the sand and small rocks. Progress was hardly noticeable. Working his fingers deeper into the sand, he scooped it aside. After a few minutes, blurry eyes revealed a mix of sand and blood on his palms. He stopped and called out for his friend. No answer. Reality couldn't be denied any longer.

Slowly, Graham returned to headquarters. "He's gone," he said when he saw Arny's expectant face.

"What happened? Why?"

"Cave-in," answered Graham. He thought a moment. "Probably poor supports for the walls and ceiling." He sat on a nearby boulder, his head in his hands and mumbled, "I should have stopped him."

Arny limped over to his friend. "It's not your fault. No one else saw the danger. Not even Jean." Arny wanted to call the other boys from tunnel A, but Graham looked very upset. He waited for what seemed like an hour before whispering, "Should we. . . Should we maybe try to reach the guys down tunnel A?"

IN THE END

After Graham's nod, Arny shuffled to the entrance of the A passageway and called out. No answer. He went in a hundred steps and tried again. No response. Graham appeared with a lantern and said he'd find them. Arny watched until the lantern light disappeared around a bend.

When Arny returned to headquarters, he realized he had nothing to do except read the journal. But at a time like this, who could read? He re-arranged the comforters so that he could elevate his foot again. For a while, he thought of times he spent with Jean. Ten months ago, Sampson had invited Jean to join their group. For the first six months, he hardly came.

For a break, Arny considered going down tunnel B to find Jean, but a sharp pain in his ankle reminded him he wouldn't last long. He started scanning the journals. He ran across a page with one of the mystery writer's haiku, one he hadn't read yet.

> *An earthquake attack,*
> *Our only route home collapsed*
> *Doorstep disaster.*

Earthquake, not what we had, thought Arny. *Our tunnel just collapsed. Jean's hope for a direct route to Vanna gone. Just like that. In a flash.* Arny looked at the haiku again. Flipping through other pages, he thought, *They must have been here a long time.* Arny remembered reading other haikus. That meant digging into already-read journals. Before putting down the pack of pages he held, he flipped through them one more time. This time he scanned for the pages with the haiku print format. He found another one.

So many tunnels,
Which way should we choose to go?
No guide. Just tough choices.

He flipped one more page back and came across another disheartening haiku.

Which way to go next,
Lost in a maze of tunnels
Painful admission.

Just where we're at.

Thinking that the haikus might be more factual than aimless musings, Arny decided to jot them down. That way he'd have something concrete to share. He dug a note pad and another pencil out of the supplies. Arny gazed around Home Base after copying the three haikus.

A jagged, odd-shaped off-white boulder caught his eye. It had been sitting by the wall, but he hadn't thought anything of it. Now it took on meaning.

The white pebbles at the base made him realize that a mystery man had been chipping pieces off that rock to use for the symbols above the tunnels. Immediately, Arny rolled over and walked to the tool area. There it was, a heavy hammer and several metal chisels. With a hammer and a medium-sized chisel, he returned to the white rock. He angled the chisel. The first hammer-chisel strike sent the rock's projection bouncing off the wall of Home Base. A stone dropped to the ground. Arny's first success quickly led to three more.

Now I don't feel so useless.

Arny didn't know if they would need the rocks for *no entry* symbols but since there wasn't any small white rocks around, it wouldn't hurt to have some handy.

When the thirty-ninth stone bounced off his knee and landed on a small pile of white rocks, Arny smiled. There was value in his work. He used eight rocks for a circle and four across the middle of the circle to communicate a *no entry* message. His smile disappeared. Arny realized he only had enough stones to make three such symbols.

Not very much, he thought. The following frustration strike carved out a larger than normal white chunk. With his thumb, he brushed a speck of dust from the bottom of his eye. Then he picked up the rock and prepared to cut it in half.

"That's what you're doing," said Graham after stepping into Home Base. Before Arny could apologize for the noise, Graham continued, "Thank God. You were our resonating light house. There were a couple of times we weren't sure which fork in the paths to take. By listening for the loudest sound in each tunnel, we were able to make the right guesses."

"Really!" said Arny, surprised.

Terry, Sampson, Perry, and Brayden followed Graham into their headquarters. He looked around relieved to be back. "Guys, should we check that cave-in? Maybe we can rescue Jean's body."

Sampson agreed. He led the way down tunnel B with the other boys following. They found one empty cart, and a few minutes later, Terry found a partially exposed shovel handle. Sampson returned to the storage area for some more shovels.

"The second cart and Jean must be buried in the gravel landslide," said Graham. "At the time of the cave-in, I'd been part way to the crevice. I was pushing the third cart to dump its contents.

Graham, Perry, Terry, and Sampson began clearing the debris. After two hours of digging, they found a cart and then Jean's hand. It took another hour before they rescued his battered body and brought it to Home Base. As they set his body on the ground, the boys from tunnel C arrived.

After they learned what happened, Len and Larry dug a grave next to Calvin's body. Using a damp cloth, Sampson wiped off some of the blood and sand from Jean's face and arms. Sampson and Terry carried Jean to the trench. They laid him along the wall next to Calvin. The boys crowded around the graves and shared their memories about Jean. The most common stories were of his independent streak and his courage to do what he thought was right. Then Perry led them in the Lord's Prayer. He concluded by asking God to restore Jean to them when they went to heaven.

"We used Calvin's cap to show where he was buried. What should we do for Jean?" Larry's question had the boys stumped. Then Larry added, "Why not use some of Arny's white stones to scribe Jean's name above his grave?" Approval followed.

"Couldn't we also put Calvin's name above his grave?" asked Sampson.

Arny said, "If we have enough. I was thinking you might want the stones for no entry symbols after you explored some side tunnels."

"Not a problem," said Perry. "Tomorrow, I'll stay back with Arny and carve out more stones for Calvin's grave. I really don't need to return to tunnel A. I've had enough of it."

"I hope we still have time to explore our passages," said Victor. "I know that Conrad and I want to learn more about which trails to follow. We *did say* that we'd check things out until midday tomorrow."

Victor's concern was seconded by Sampson and Brayden. They wanted to learn more about the paths in tunnel A. With confirmation of the original plan, the boys returned to Home Base for a serving of Sampson's fries and a good night's rest. All but one lantern was dimmed. Time to think about their circumstances and the loss of Jean and the loss of Calvin. What more dangers were in store for them? Time to think of home.

Curled up in his sleeping bag, Perry's thoughts turned to Jean's prediction that there was little chance of being rescued. *He was right,* thought Perry. *There's no chance.* Perry remembered hearing the garage crash down the sink hole shortly after he had pinned his map to one of the sleeping bags and left. He hurried back to find his path blocked. The sides of the tunnel had collapsed. Access to the sinkhole was gone. *Rescuers on a recovery mission wouldn't see a sign of a tunnel in which the boys might have escaped in. They'd just continue to point their lights down the hole looking for the garage.*

After returning to Home Base, Perry signaled Victor to join him in the kitchen area. In a low voice he reported the collapse and asked Victor if the others should be told. Victor told him there was no point.

Then Perry confessed, "We're all going to die in here."

Victor had looked at him in shock. "You! The one most of us look to for unwavering faith are afraid to go to heaven?" It took a few moments before Perry shook his head and then smiled. He recalled a position he'd taken in a conversation about facing death. "You have to think that heaven is a place of perfection. A whole lot better than what we have now. What's to worry about?"

When Victor left, Perry hung back for a few seconds and prayed for the Lord to strengthen his faith.

Before closing his eyes, Perry repeated the prayer.

Wake-up time came with the clattering of pans in the kitchen area where Sampson and Perry were making enough pancakes to carry the boys for most of the day. Sampson's eager start was spurred by an intended surprise for his friends. In the supplies of the mystery men he had found dried apples chips. He soaked and then added them to the pancake mix for flavoring. "Better than yesterday's day's flavoring," he expected to hear.

"You surprised me last night," began Sampson as he mixed his batter.

"What do you mean?" asked Perry.

"You didn't want to go back into tunnel A."

"Yeah, well, I don't feel comfortable in there."

"Why not?"

"Well, this may sound a bit crazy, but I have a strange feeling in there, like some presence is waiting for us to make a mistake, waiting to kill us."

"You sure that you're not letting Calvin's and Jean's deaths spook you?" Sampson quit mixing the batter and looked carefully at his friend.

"I didn't even know about Jean at the time. I just felt a deep-bone coldness in there. I know it wasn't cold, but that's the sensation that crept over me as we walked in. It makes no sense. It made me think of death. That's why I didn't say anything, and don't you tell anyone either."

"I won't," Sampson agreed as he reassured Perry. "I take it that you will be in favor of us taking the C route when it comes time to leave Home Base?

"If we still agree to all leave together."

CHAPTER 8

A Critical Decision

Len, Larry, Victor, and Conrad returned to the little lake near the waterfall. Scaling the side of the fissure proved to be no problem for them. Before exploring the many slopes that they found, they topped up with cold water.

Two factors guided their choice: go up and choose an easy route to walk. At times, they needed to backtrack to find a new path across a sharp divide or an impossible-to-climb obstruction. Len and Larry loved these challenges, thinking of it as working their way through a corn maze.

Victor found their situation disturbing. The sun felt energizing. Its light cast a feeling of hope, of optimism. When walking in open spaces, the June sun's rays brought images of tanning on the beach. That feeling changed dramatically when he walked along the rocky inclines or climbed its steep slopes, and there were many such slopes. Heat radiating from the rocks created an oven atmosphere.

He could manage that discomfort. But where were the birds? And no trees, no shade. That was disquieting. More troubling was the sand displayed no plant life, no insects.

The absence of life bade an unsettling message. This is a place of death. You shouldn't be here.

He searched the blue sky. No planes. No sign of human life. Maybe we're in a no-fly zone. His attention shifted to the top of the mountain. *The surface shouldn't be that far up,* he thought. *If we reach the top, we'll be at ground level, level where the garage once sat. From there, I'm sure we could find our way home.* That motivated him to offer encouragement.

Conrad enjoyed the adventure of prowling in the sun. Climbing was always a challenge he welcomed, but here he was concerned about getting lost. He had visions of a person aimlessly wandering around in a desert and of dying of thirst. He had two water bottles hooked to his belt. To control the fear of being lost, he focused on Victor.

Len, Larry, Victor, and Conrad had no clear hope that scaling this area would bring them home. All that was certain was sore muscles and heat. Their report at the midday meeting offered an uncertain hope of getting home by using their daylight option. For the rest of the boys, the ache of sore muscles from working on the ramp carried a lot of weight. Who wanted to exert a lot of effort climbing under a hot sun?

Sampson's investigation was no more inviting. He described their area as one like walking inside of a giant anthill. Tunnels were everywhere. Some were tall, enabling the boys to walk upright. Many involved bending. Some required crawling. In most places, the shoring was nonexistent or crumbling. Because of the weight from above, he hoped that compacted clay and gravel would remain stable if undisturbed.

"Good. That means no more digging," said Terry.

When the snickering ended, Sampson continued, "Even walkable tunnels were confusing. Go right or left. Those going upward ended on a gentle slope down, some ending in sharp drops others in cave-ins."

Twice they discovered they had gone in a circle. Because they stayed together, many possible routes remained unexplored. When they encountered forks, they used a half dozen of Arny's white rocks to indicate the tunnel they left and the new fork they were entering. Then they ran out of the stones. Sampson chose the right fork. That way on the way back they knew where to go. The most common feature of almost all the passages was that they headed downward. The greater the descent, the greater the dampness. Returning home was a lost cause.

Arny's response to Sampson's concern was to share a few haikus that the mystery writer left about Vanna. He read:

> *Deep in a dark mine*
> *Remember Vanna*

IN THE END

My prime lifeline hope.

and

Fishing canoeing,
Paddleboats and water skis
My water-fun home.

and

Drama festivals,
Flourishing art galleries
Passion lover's home.

"Vanna doesn't sound so bad, guys. At times it sounds like a holiday resort. There's more, but I think you get the idea." Arny looked for acceptance among his listeners.

Conrad cleared his throat for attention. "I agree with Arny. Vanna sounds good. Of course, my first choice is to get back home, but I honestly don't see that in our future. Tunnel A heads down not up. That's not the way home. Tunnel C's steep slopes may lead us home but in some places it looks dangerous. I don't like either one, but we have to get out of here soon. Our food, or the mystery men's food supply won't last much longer. I'm willing to go with whatever the group decides."

Victor patted his friend on the back. "Good analysis. I'd like to say your gloomy forecast sounded like your usual pessimistic self. Your conclusion is the key. We must act soon. I confess I'm not like a bat. Hanging around in caves is not my thing. I prefer the daylight. There's a whole lot more to see, but I will go with the majority."

"I think that we should choose tunnel A." Terry's choice had everyone's attention. "Listening to Conrad, I hear that it's pretty hot out there. In tunnel A, we don't have that problem. We will have to ration our light use. We don't know how long we'll be in the dark, and we have a limited supply of kerosene. I only hope that we aren't in the tunnels for too long. We only have a few batteries for our flashlights. The good thing is those are problems we can manage."

Brayden's raised voice proclaimed his conviction. "No way I go with tunnel C. The climb up the fissure is enough to convince me. I can't handle that area. Sure, we have a rope. I might make it up the first challenge. If we're faced with other climbing encounters like that, I won't be able to handle it. You'd have no choice but to leave me behind or return back for our tunnel A option. So, I say, start with tunnel A."

In a response, Perry stated, "Tunnel A gives me the creeps. Didn't you see the number of graves that we came across? People were dying in there for some reason. I really don't want to find out why. I just don't want anything to do with it."

Victor added another objection that he almost forgot. "The A option has so many branch tunnels and forks. We could be wandering around in the dark forever."

"Hey, guys. This sounds like we won't be going together. Is that what we are driving at?" Larry's observation stopped conversation for a few minutes.

"We have our preferences," began Sampson, "but are they so strong that we'll let them divide us?

I was thinking, is there any one important factor that we need to consider, one that might help us come to a decision?"

Silenced once again. Then Graham said, "Sounds like you have one in mind."

"If we're going to stay together, then I think we should consider what route Arny can best manage. tunnel C sounds like it would prevent Arny from coming with us."

"I'll do my best no matter what you guys decide." Arny smiled. Others nodded their approval. It's what they expected.

"It's not your intention that concerns me," responded Sampson, walking up to his friend. "Which route would cause a greater strain on your foot?" Looking at Arny, he added, "We don't want to add to your pain. You've endured enough already, unless you're looking for an excuse to do more reading" —he pointed to the paper booklet close to Arny's hand —"or maybe you plan to start writing your own journal."

"Sampson has a point." Len walked up to Arny. "Don't think I'm trying to put you down, but I have to admit that the areas we have walked are rugged. Sure, you'd try to handle it, but over time your injured foot would slow you down, maybe even make progress impossible." Facing the rest of the boys, Len said, "Like Victor, I would really like to stay with the daylight setting but I'm willing to go with tunnel A for Arny's sake."

"I agree," said Larry.

Each of the boys stated that they would accept tunnel A.

"Guess what?" asked Arny. No one said anything. "We sound like a group that would really fit into the Vanna community. Listen to this. It's the last haiku that the mystery writer penned." He read:

One large family.
Everyone cares for the other guy.
Close community.

"Good one," said Larry. "Some time you'll have to read the other haikus."

"Just to make it clear," said Conrad. "From now on, our mission is to find this fictional Vanna." He paused. "Not try to get home."

"Fictional! I didn't say that, did I?" Arny's immediate response caught everyone's attention. His brow furrowed. He looked carefully at his friends.

"No. But we really don't know if this place exists. We just have that writer's word for it," said Conrad.

"Whatever," said Sampson. "We're going to try and find this place, right, guys?"

A chorus of yeahs responded.

Sampson pointed out that if they wanted to act on their decision tomorrow morning, there was some packing and organizing to do. Victor volunteered to help Sampson. Arny and Perry turned to making more stone markers. Len and Conrad picked up all the empty water bottles and a couple of jugs. They headed to the lake to fill them up. Larry took a small pail of stones to Calvin and Jean's graves. There he imprinted their names on the wall above their respective graves.

After a little more than two hours, Arny came to the kitchen area. Victor and Sampson were grouping supplies for each person to carry. Arny needed a break from chipping at the boulder. Sampson pointed to one of the two backpacks on ground. The small one loaded with extra flashlights and batteries was for Arny.

Sampson told Arny to stick to the middle of the group. He could use one of the lanterns so that he could see where he was stepping. Sampson reviewed what each grouping of supplies held. He planned to carry the heaviest backpack, the one with the food and some pans. When he found Brayden's bag, he said he had to confirm that Brayden would take the Coleman stove and other cooking utensils. He also wanted to ask Brayden to help him lead the way through the tunnels. Brayden was the most familiar with the tunnels, at least with those nearest to Home Base.

As soon as Sampson left, Victor felt a light tap on his shoulder. He turned and saw Arny with his index finger to his lips. Arny glanced around to make sure that no one else was near. Then leaning closer to Victor, he whispered. "I didn't really suggest to anyone that this writer's work was a fiction, did I?"

Victor shook his head. "Why?"

Again, Arny looked around. Still in a low voice, he said, "Lately I've been wondering. He wrote some things that seem to be too good to be true."

"What makes you think that?"

Arny paused. When Victor said nothing, he continued, "He wrote something like what I think was a love letter. I think he was practicing what he might say to her. Anyway, she sounded fantastic, unbelievable. I would love to meet her."

"I suppose a guy in love could see someone like that."

"Then there were other stories about amazingly caring, helpful people. You'd think the whole community was a church."

"A kind of heavenly place?"

"Yeah."

"Well, if I was you, I'd keep those stories to yourself. When we find out that these tunnels are leading us nowhere, we may need to hear some of those good stories about Vanna to keep us going. To keep our spirits up."

Arny and Victor were almost finished packing the bags when Sampson returned.

"Arny," said Sampson, "did you have something on your mind when you came back here?"

"An idle thought," said Arny. "In your travels through the tunnels, did you happen to see any other books or papers, you know, like the journal that was left here? Maybe something left by the grave sides?"

"No," answered Sampson. "Why?"

"I was thinking that those mystery men must have gone through what we are doing now, choosing which route to follow, packing supplies. My writer friend didn't say anything about that. Now I have no other information on how well they did. Did he make it to Vanna? Did he die along the route? I really don't know what happened to him."

"You're right. We don't know how they made out. I didn't see anything in the tunnels except those rock messages to indicate if they were successful."

"I was hoping that my writer friend would have written something about their walk home. If you didn't come across one of his writings, then maybe he made it back." Seeing Sampson take a breath to say something, Arny added, "I know this is all hopeful thinking. He may not have made it."

"Probably best not to bring this up with the others. Don't want them to start worrying," said Sampson.

"Or to second-guess their decision," added Victor. "I can see Conrad thinking our tunnel A has doomed us to failure."

"And Perry is so spooked by tunnel A. I've convinced him to stick close to me when we are in the tunnels. That way I can try to handle his concerns. We don't need to give him more reason to doubt our decision."

CHAPTER 9

Just What the Doctor Ordered

The next morning, the boys left the cavern. Sampson started their trek with, "Be sure not to touch the shoring. Even though they are in poor shape, they may be all that's preventing the walls from caving in."

The first hour they walked two abreast, then dropped to single file. The tunnel narrowed but remained high enough for them to walk upright. Their progress impressed most of the boys. They thought checking out tunnel A was the right choice. Sampson and Brayden were unimpressed. They'd walked the route before.

In the third hour, Conrad called out. He wanted to explore a tunnel on his left, a little narrower but the same height. It was the first upward leading tunnel they had encountered. *A possible route home,* he thought.

Sampson disagreed and said they should push on. He and Brayden hadn't explored beyond this point. "This is the main tunnel. It should lead somewhere important. If it comes to a dead end, then we can start exploring side tunnels."

Reluctantly, Conrad accepted Sampson's logic. He let the other boys pass him. Then he piled six rocks at the entrance of the tunnel with the incline.

Half an hour later, and the boys came to a fork. Branches to the right and left were of the same width and height. Without hesitation Sampson, chose the right side. Everyone followed without a second thought. Everyone except Len and Larry.

Since Terry had been on all the explorations with Sampson before, Len reached out and tapped him on the shoulder. Terry stopped and turned around.

"Why did he go right?" asked Len.

"It's his pattern," explained Terry. "In the beginning, we had no pattern. Sometimes we'd go right, other times left. When we had to backtrack we couldn't remember which way we chose earlier. After returning back to a familiar route, Sampson said if the tunnels in a fork are similar, we should always choose one direction. He chose the right. That way when we backtracked, we knew which way to go."

"Logical," said Larry.

"You said if the tunnels in the fork were similar?" persisted Len. He signaled Terry to join him by the left-leading tunnel.

"Yeah."

"But here they aren't."

"What do you mean?" asked Terry as he came closer to Len who was standing at the fork and pointing to the left option.

"Look twenty feet ahead." Len pointed his flashlight down the tunnel. "See. It widens, and it's heading downward."

"Maybe Sampson didn't shine the light down this tunnel. He just automatically went right," explained Terry with a shrug of his shoulders.

"But he should've felt the breeze from this tunnel. Can't you feel it in your face?" Len stepped back a little so that Terry could step in front of the tunnel entrance.

"You're right. Guess he missed it." Terry moved back.

"I think we should check it out. That breeze suggests open air. Could be like tunnel C. Who knows? Maybe it opens up to this Vanna."

Terry saw their group almost twenty feet away. "I'll catch Sampson. He may go with your idea."

As Terry turned to leave Len stopped him. "Let him plow ahead. Larry and I will check this out. We won't be long."

"But we're supposed to stick together." Terry faced Len again.

Len took six rocks from the pocket of his jacket. On the ground he set three rocks from the tunnel they were in and the other three down the new tunnel, the indicators the group had agreed to use when they explored branch tunnels.

Looking up at Terry, he said, "Now you know where we went. If our tunnel comes to a dead end, we'll catch up with the rest of you. We'll remember how Sampson is picking his way."

Terry shrugged and glanced at the group. They were becoming harder to see. He had no flashlight. If he was going to catch up, he had to leave now. Bouncing off the sides of the tunnel in the dark was not an option.

"Go ahead," said Len, shining his flashlight at the disappearing group. Terry hurried off. When darkness enveloped Terry's body, Len said, "Shall we?"

Larry nodded and followed after his friend. When the tunnel widened, he walked alongside Len. They came to a branch tunnel. The one to the right was much narrower. The height lower. It was the source of the breeze. Len bent down and placed six rocks on the ground to indicate that they were continuing straight ahead. The sign was necessary. Their friends might have used the breeze as a guideline. More branch tunnels appeared. They were smaller, half the height of the main tunnel. Len put no rocks down. Pointing down the tunnel, he said, "Common sense."

The farther down the tunnel they traveled, the more they noticed the tunnel widening. Moisture hung heavy in the air. The walls were wet, no circulating air. They stopped to catch their breath, to debate continuing farther. Larry's stomach gurgled.

"Hungry?" asked Len.

"One meal a day is for the birds." Larry shook his head.

Victor had convinced the group to ration their food. They agreed on eating breakfast only. This morning Sampson reduced the number of pancakes he served.

"There's no burger in sight, but I could sure go for one," said Larry. A smile lit up his face. "I can almost smell it now."

"Know what you mean," said Len. "It's like driving by a KFC restaurant. My mouth waters. I always want to go in."

They each took in a deep breath. An enchanting smell encouraged them to breathe it in more deeply. Disbelief caused them to do it again. They looked at each other, faces beaming. With a nod, they turned. A mission pace marked their walk down the tunnel.

"I love the smell of food, any food," added Larry. "Especially mustard."

"Yes, mustard," said Len. They each pictured a foot-long hot dog, one loaded with relish and mustard. "Makes me think of a baseball game, intermission, hot dogs, and fries."

"Nothing's better than that," said Len.

"See it?" asked Larry as they rounded the bend in the tunnel. A ray of daylight pierced the darkness. Larry pointed straight ahead and a little upward. "See the sign?"

"Just what we need," said Len, looking at a hot dog advertisement.

I can hardly wait to get there and sink my teeth into it."

"Me too," said Len, drooling. "Race you."

"You're on," said Larry. He broke into a run.

"Last one there pays," said Len charging from behind. The spirit of competition drove him to pass his Larry. He glanced back at his laughing friend and then forward again. His focus was on the hot dog on the sign. He was going to get there first. No doubt.

Then to his surprise, the sign began rising higher and higher. Len's legs pumped faster. He had to get that dog before it disappeared. The hot dog rose farther and farther away. A floating feeling overwhelmed Len. He wished for jets strapped to his back so they could propel him up to the hot dog, so close to the hot dog that he could reach out and grab it. The sign continued to distance itself from him. Pain stabbed his feet. It raced up his back. A sharp pain stung his face so hard that all he experienced was darkness, total darkness, then nothing. Like Len, Larry followed.

***

Terry thought of squeezing past Victor and Conrad. They were carrying sleeping bags. It was impossible. Then there was Arny. *Can't bump him.* Terry expected that Sampson would call for a break soon, for Arny's sake. *That's when I'll tell Sampson about Len and Larry,* he thought. Terry didn't have more than twenty minutes to wait. *Finally*, he thought. He stepped over the resting bodies.

"They what?" exclaimed Sampson when he heard of Larry and Len's action. He swallowed some water and said, "They should have just piled some rocks at that junction so that we could check it out later."

He looked at his seated friends. They needed their break, their talk. After five minutes, he asked Brayden to take over leading the group. "Start in about twenty minutes. Go slowly and follow our same pattern." He explained he was worried about Larry and Len. He and Terry would go back and find their missing friends.

Graham heard the conversation and insisted on going with Sampson. "If they're seriously hurt, you'll need some help, especially if someone has to be carried."

"In that case," said Conrad, "I'm coming." When Sampson started to shake his head, Conrad added, "Me and Terry to carry Len, and you and Graham to carry Larry."

"He's right," added Graham.

"Okay. Okay. We'll leave our stuff here. And you guys—"

"I'll stay with our things," said Arny. He looked at Brayden and Perry. "And, if you want, you can investigate the tunnels around here."

Brayden nodded. Perry sensed something was seriously wrong. He stayed quiet lest his voice showed his fear.

Sampson started back. He had no trouble finding Len and Larry's six-stone marker. He focused on scuff mark signs on the ground to confirm his friends had passed this way. When they came to the tunnel and the rocks on the ground, Terry expressed surprise.

"Len said that the breeze might lead to an opening, to daylight. I would have thought he'd have continued following it."

Shining the light into the branch tunnel, Sampson said, "Ground looks uneven in there. Tougher going. Looks like he chose the easier way."

"Or maybe he thought he was on the main passageway," said Graham. "Look at the cartwheels tracks imbedded in the ground."

"Could be," said Sampson.

When they came to other smaller branch tunnels, they stopped and checked each to see if there was any sign that Len and Larry left the main route. "In case they split up," said Sampson. "Never know what they will do."

While Graham and Sampson were spending a little more time examining the ground and sides of one of the small branch tunnels, Terry ducked. Then he ducked again and stepped back into Conrad.

"Hey. Watch it," said a surprised Conrad. His attention was focused on what was behind them. At first, he thought it was a small dog then a cat. He decided it was neither, but it was some kind of small creature. And fast. It sought to remain in the shadows.

Graham turned around. "What's the matter?"

Peering above him, Terry said, "There's a bat here. Maybe more than one. It dive-bombed me, twice." He continued looking around expecting another attack.

Sampson turned attention to his friends. "What do you mean?"

Conrad held up his lantern and pointed to the tunnel behind him and explained that they were being stalked by some small dark creature. He put a hand on the wall so he wouldn't fall.

Sampson squinted, seeing Conrad's action. Then he shone his light down the tunnel. After a moment, he said, "There's nothing there."

"There is. I'm telling you. I saw it. It moves very fast." His serious voice convinced Sampson to shine his light back down the tunnel again. Conrad took a couple of steps back. He unbuttoned his shirt. Seeing Graham's questioning look, he said, "I'm hot."

"Nothing there. It's your imagination." Sampson returned.

"Hey," said Graham. "Hand me the light." He examined the sides and the top of the tunnel. He had seen Terry quickly duck as if he were about to be attacked. "Bats," he whispered to Graham.

"No bats," he said to Terry.

"There are." Fear marked Terry's response.

"What's going on here?" asked Sampson, frustrated.

"We've got to get out of here. Now," said Terry. He managed three steps back before Conrad grabbed him.

"No. It's not safe." Conrad's remark forced Terry to stop.

Sampson shone his light back in the direction that they had come. He saw no sign of danger. He turned to Graham and saw a furrowed brow.

Then Graham leaned closer to Sampson and whispered, "We've got to get out of here now." He pointed in the direction from which they came. "Grab Conrad. I'll take Terry."

Sampson stood in disbelief. *Is everyone going crazy?* He checked Graham's face. *No sign of fear. Not like Terry or Conrad. He looks sane, serious.*

"Let's go. Now." Graham's voice broke through Sampson's thoughts.

Sampson grabbed Conrad. Conrad resisted. "Don't worry," said Sampson, pulling Conrad. "Our light will scare your creature away." He made progress. Graham followed with Terry in tow.

After passing the tunnel with light breeze, Graham called out. "I think we can stop."

Sampson shone his light at each of his friends. Fear had disappeared from their faces. Terry and Conrad stood quietly, breathing heavily but saying nothing. Looking at Graham, he mouthed, "What's going on?" Graham signaled him to come closer.

"My best guess. Terry and Conrad were hallucinating. The only thing I can think of is a gas, an odorless, tasteless gas."

"A gas? Like laughing gas?"

Graham nodded.

"What makes you think so?"

"I don't really know, but Conrad and Terry weren't faking. What they saw was real to them. They were afraid. I'm guessing Conrad felt a little dizzy. That's why he reached to the wall to steady himself. And Terry was sweating. Those are side effects of nitrous oxide."

"But we weren't affected?"

"Maybe because we were poking around in the side tunnel at the time. Given a little more time, we could have experienced the same thing. That's why I said we had to get out of there fast."

"So, we're okay here?"

"Because of that side tunnel's breeze, we are receiving fresh air, oxygen. That should mean we are okay. I expect Conrad and Terry will be normal soon too."

Conrad and Terry sat on the ground their backs against the wall. Neither spoke.

"They look drained," said Sampson.

"Possible side effect."

After a brief pause, Sampson said, "You stay here with them. Take care of them. I'm going back to see if I can find Len and Larry. I hope they're sitting—"

"You can't." The pitch of Graham's voice caused Terry and Conrad to look up.

Sampson's hand shot up to silence Graham. "Don't worry. I won't poke around the side tunnels. I'll hurry down the main tunnel."

"But you don't know how far it is. You could fall under the influence of the gas too."

"I tell you what. First sign of hallucinations, and I'll come back. I'll run back."

"Sampson." Again, Graham's voice drew the attention of their sitting friends.

Pointing to Conrad and Terry, Sampson said, "I have to go. Len and Larry could be sitting on the ground like them. They will need someone to grab them and bring them back. Don't worry. I'll be careful."

"Okay. Be careful, very careful."

Sampson hurried back. Shortly after passing the tunnel with the breeze, he noted the air was heavier, moister. Some spots on the wall showed clinging drops of water. Sampson's walk continued uninterrupted until he came to a deep cavern.

No place to go. No Larry. No Len. Did I miss a sign of them turning off? Did they neglect to leave me a sign?

Sampson looked down. At first, he saw nothing. A faint shining light beamed on to a wall. Sampson followed the light to its source. Nothing. His light scanned the area around the light. Then he saw it—two bodies draped over rocks. Len and Larry over fifty feet below.

He screamed to them. No response. Sampson refused to believe it was real. His friends. . . dead. He squatted and slammed his fist into the ground. The pain was real. The bodies below were real. He checked to see if there was any hope of recovering their bodies, but the drop was too steep, too far down. Sampson sunk to the ground, his head buried in his hands, his body shaking. Wonderful memories of Larry and Len washed over him.

"What do I do?" he whispered. In response, he imagined Perry seated beside him saying to pray. Sampson silently cried, then mumbled the Lord's Prayer. When opened his eyes, he looked to his left expecting to see Perry beside him. He wasn't.

Did I imagine Perry here?

He reviewed the last few minutes.

Did I hallucinate?

He shook his head.

But would I know if I was seeing things?

He recalled his words to Graham. "First sign of hallucinations, and I'll come back. I'll run back." He stood up, looked down at the remains of Len and Larry, and then hurried away.

CHAPTER 10

What You Want

The late afternoon sun beat down on Victor, Brayden, Perry, and Arny. Heat radiating from the rocks warmed them. They stood admiring the view below. A blue stream crossed a mostly barren rocky floor. Green shrubs and reeds bordered both sides of the running water. The precipitous drop from their perch prevented them from sliding down, but they couldn't ignore the tantalizing invitation from the oasis which seemed to say, "Come. I'm just what you want."

Victor pointed to a high plateau in the distance. He thought he'd seen it before from a lookout point coming out of the tunnel C. The partial view of the mesa jutting up from the floor made him wish he were a bird.

If only I could be there, he thought. *From such a vantage point, I might be able to see a way out of the barren rocks, maybe even see Vanna.*

For him, reaching that mesa meant working a way down to the gully floor and then tackling a mammoth climbing venture.

Must be a better alternative to get to the mesa, Victor thought.

Victor heard steps behind him. He saw Sampson and the others approach. The absence of Larry and Len pulled the boys from their enchanting view. Sampson broke the news—Larry and Len are dead. He described the scene.

Arny refused to believe Len and Larry were really gone. He wanted to go to the crevasse and see them for himself.

Graham was alarmed. "It's too dangerous." He explained what he thought had happened.

Gas, thought Perry. *More like the devil himself waiting for an opportunity to snatch us. I knew these tunnels were dangerous. We've got to get out of here.*

Victor shook his head in disbelief. Brayden stood silent, shocked.

The boys went back to retrieve their possessions and returned to the rocky perch. It was wide enough for them to sit in a circle. There, they talked about the fun they had with Larry and Len. At Victor's request Perry led the boys in another memorial service.

During the service, Sampson said nothing. He wondered if there was anything, he could have done to prevent the tragedy. He saw himself as a shepherd who lost two of his sheep to a wolf.

The late afternoon heat soon brought yawns. While some boys stretched out on their sleeping bags, Victor returned to the spot where he could gaze down at the valley. Terry and Conrad followed.

"That narrow strip of green," said Victor, talking out loud to no one, "must mean that there is something better to look forward to."

Terry and Conrad eagerly speculated about Victor's hope. Their enthusiasm lead to discussing plans for tomorrow.

"What passageway should we explore next?" asked Terry.

"Not what passageway, what passageways. Instead of sticking together as a group, we need to split up and check as many tunnels as possible."

"I agree," said Arny as he joined them. "We'll never get out here if we look at one tunnel at a time."

"Anything that cuts down the time we spend poking around in the darkness," said Terry.

Arny limped to Brayden and Graham. Both were stretched out on their sleeping bag, eyes closed, recovering from their trials. Arny tapped the bottom of Brayden's foot. When he opened his eyes, Arny said, "What do you think?" He paused. "About each of us checking out as many tunnels as possible tomorrow?"

"Sounds okay to me."

Arny nudged Graham, awakening him. Graham said, "You're saying we should feel free to explore any tunnel we want."

"Yes," confirmed Arny.

"If that's the case, we have to inform the rest of the group about where we are going. We don't want to lose track of each other."

"Or at least inform one person to keep track of who is where," said Arny.

Conrad looked to Sampson, but Sampson was wondering if it would have made any difference if Len and Larry had been close to him and Brayden. *It would have been easy for them to question my decision to go right.*

Conrad saw Victor standing on edge of the ridge, looking down. *Probably searching for some way down,* he thought.

"Then it's decided," announced Conrad. "We'll hit as many tunnels as we can."

Conrad looked at Brayden and Graham. They'd already closed their eyes.

They're tired, thought Conrad.

Victor and Sampson were both lost in thought. He then looked at Terry who nodded his approval.

"Guess I'll explore the tunnel that I left the stone markers at, agreed?" Conrad pointed to a place in the sun where he and Terry could sit.

"Right," said Terry.

"You know why I want to check that particular tunnel, don't you?" Conrad made himself comfortable.

"Why?"

"The incline."

"You still think we can find a way to the surface? I thought we gave up on that possibility a long time ago."

"I guess I really would like to go home. If there's any possibility, I have to check it out. I miss my family. Don't you?"

Terry and Conrad's conversation focused on special family members. Across from them Perry sat in silence, overwhelmed by the futility of their circumstances.

There is no way out of here. We'll be roaming around the bowels of this underground labyrinth like the Jews who wandered in the desert for forty years. What's the use of trying to get out of here? The penalty is death.

For a while, his attention shifted to Calvin, Jean, Len, and Larry. Then he heard a segment of Terry and Conrad's conversation. Perry's father came to mind.

What would he say to me now?

The answer came instantly. "Pray." In times of trouble, he always said, "Don't be afraid to take it to the Lord. Ask for his blessing, his guidance, his strength. You'll be glad you did." Perry closed his eyes. "Lord, I'm in trouble. I need your help. Grant me the strength, the wisdom I need to get me through this terrible trial." That's the last Perry could recall before he fell asleep.

***

Sampson started the next morning by making pancakes. The air was cool, but the sun was bright. The boys were optimistic after a good night's rest.

Sampson regretted not paying attention to Terry, Arny, and Conrad when they had discussed the plans for the new day. His focus had returned to Conrad's "then it's decided." He'd thought, *Too late to say anything now.* Thoughts of Larry and Len's death refused to let him go.

Sampson brought a plate of pancakes.

Perry was saying, "Maybe I can sketch a map to show which tunnels we went through."

"And we should each check our own tunnel," said Brayden. "That way more tunnels are looked at."

"As we find them," clarified Graham. "That way we don't miss a tunnel."

Burning the candle at both ends, thought Sampson. *Even if they go in pairs, their plan means all the lanterns and the flashlights will be used at the same time. Before long, they'll be in the dark. Then what?* Sampson said nothing. To him, his failure to look out for Len and Larry meant he wasn't fit to be a leader.

As the plate was being passed around, Conrad said, "Well, I know what I want to do. There was a place that I piled six rocks at an entrance. It was before Len and Larry's turn off. Anyway, I want to check that tunnel first if I can find it."

"I have an idea where it is," said Sampson. He had counted tunnel mouths before they came to the fork. "I'll help you find it."

IN THE END

Victor suggested they should travel in pairs for greater safety. Everyone agreed. With the exception of Conrad, the rest would explore the tunnels as they appeared and report their findings to Perry. He'd record everything on a map. They also decided to leave their supplies at the landing where they slept. Returning to daylight meant they had a reward to look forward to.

Shortly after beginning their walk, the boys came upon a narrow opening to their left. Graham and Brayden volunteered to check that passage. A few hundred steps farther, another tunnel branched off. Victor and Terry paired off. When they came to the next tunnel, Arny volunteered to check it. "Gentle incline, level ground. Something my foot can handle," he said. Perry sat on the ground and began sketching a new map.

Conrad and Sampson went ahead. Their search took longer than Conrad expected. Sampson's confidence kept them going.

Six light-colored stones. They found Conrad's tunnel. Narrow. Uneven ground. Conrad took the lead, advancing slowly. Unfilled holes were everywhere. Sometimes going was so tight that they had to walk sideways, but the trek was always upward. Sometimes the incline was very steep.

Wouldn't have been good for Arny, thought Sampson.

When their passageway reduced to a crawl space, Sampson suggested they return to Perry. Conrad refused to quit. He thought he could see a light at the end of the tunnel. How far away, he wasn't certain. He had to crawl to reach the end. Sampson waited for him.

The crawl became more challenging than Conrad anticipated. Many rocks were sharp. It meant carefully placing his hands and his knees on rough surfaces. Occasionally, he dislodged sharp surfaces with a nearby loose rock. Other times, he'd brush loose debris from the walls to partially cover a sharp surface. After inching forward for twenty feet, he considered giving up. He changed his mind when he saw the tunnel widening. Eventually, he was able to half squat to move ahead. When he could stand straight up, he called back to Sampson. His friend declined to follow him unless there was something more than a large opening to see. The next time Conrad reported back, the daylight was real, and he discovered a different perspective of the valley floor. His discovery convinced Sampson to brave the trials of Conrad's passageway.

"Beautiful," said Sampson, looking at an elevated plateau in the distance. One side of the plateau was a sheer drop, the other a graveled slope and a stream racing down to a valley floor. *Victor should see this.* Large boulders of various sizes littered the valley floor below them. Three crow-sized birds flew past him and landed on the rocky face to his right. He noticed several nests.

Eggs! Great! he thought. *Maybe. Got to try.*

Studying the wall to the side of him and the nests, he noted wide ledges that would easily hold his weight. There were enough ridges to reach three of the five bird nests.

He stuck his hands in his jacket pockets to see if he had room for the eggs. Six marker stones. He'd brought them to show the others which tunnel he and Conrad had taken. Instead, he used the stones that Conrad had left when Sampson had insisted that they continue straight ahead together. Sampson gave his stones to Conrad.

"How does scrambled eggs for supper sound?" he asked Conrad. "May only be a few bites."

"Super." Conrad's exclamation erased Sampson's lingering doubt.

Sampson studied the wall, planning where each step would take place. "Got to be careful," he murmured. After one last look at Conrad, Sampson stepped out on the ledge. He stood still for a few moments feeling the sturdiness beneath his feet.

The standard protocol, he thought.

His progress was measured with the same caution. Firm foundation. Key. The eggs weren't worth risking his life for. The distance to the first nest was about twenty-three feet. The first ten feet caused no doubts. Another five feet. Sampson felt like a fly on the wall. Such pests on the wall in his study he'd swat. Sampson checked both sides of him.

No giant ready to swat me.

After another four feet, a bird noticed Sampson's presence. Its squawks left Sampson uneasy. Would she fly away or defend her nest? Another three feet. Sampson heard flapping wings. Eyeing his target,

Sampson edged forward another foot. The brownish-colored bird flew out of the nest. Sampson froze, expecting an attack. Maybe it would dive at him, strike the back of his head, or worse, strike his face. Nothing happened. Sampson stretched his leg a foot and a half away for the next foothold. Nothing. He transferred his weight to his left foot.

Incoming.

A shadow on the wall's face. The mother darted within six inches of his face.

Shot across the bow, thought Sampson. *A warning? Will she strike me next time?*

Sampson's legs bent slightly, preparing to absorb the expected impact. Keeping one hand against the cliff's wall, he freed the other hand to deflect a potential attack. Sampson stood still. No new shadows on the wall's face. One more step and he could reach into the nest and find eggs. He slid his foot slowly, making sure it was firmly in place before the weight transfer. His hand shot up. Somewhere above, the mother screeched. Sampson picked two eggs.

Kind of small, he thought.

He quickly put them in his pocket. Again, he reached. Two more eggs.

That's all.

Sampson looked back at Conrad and received a thumbs-up.

Enough for an appetizer, he thought. *The guys will love this.*

Sampson turned his attention to the next nest four feet away, but not as high up. Again, before moving, he tested each foothold to make certain it would hold the rest of his weight. The mother in the next nest squawked sooner, louder than the ones before. She flapped her wings more furiously too. When he was within a foot of the nest, she flew off. His reward—five eggs. He signaled his find to Conrad.

Now one more nest, the last nest. Five more eggs, and we'll each have two eggs for supper, a surprise supper.

Sampson looked at the nest five feet away. He checked where he would be placing his feet. The steps were reasonably close.

Should be no trouble.

Again, exercising all the care he used in approaching the other two nests, Sampson worked his way closer to his next reward. Two feet away. Nothing changed. The mother screeched and furiously beat her wings. A darting shadow flashed onto the face of the cliff. Sampson semi-squatted, expecting an impact.

Mother's mate.

No impact. After waiting a long time for an attack, Sampson edged closer to the last nest. The mother flew off. Sampson breathed a sigh of relief. He looked at the last step he'd have to take for the eggs.

Easy.

He glanced back at all the steps he'd taken so far. Amazing. He had imagined each step, each foothold perfectly.

And the guys thought I'd lost my powers of keen observation. Wait 'till they hear about this. Then they'll know I'm fit to be a good leader.

With the same care as before, Sampson took his last step toward the nest. No problem. He looked around and saw two growing shadows on the rock's face. He raised his right hand to fend off the expected impact to the back of his head. The first shadow hit his hand.

Thank God.

Feathers from the wing of the second shadow swept Sampson's face below his eyes. Instinctively, he threw his head back. His heels sought support to hold him upright. There was none. A second later, Sampson was looking at the blue sky. A sky rapidly slipping farther and farther away. He screamed.

Conrad screamed.

Sharp pain stabbed Sampson's back. It was sharper than he'd ever felt. Then he heard nothing. Saw nothing. Felt nothing.

Conrad stood shocked. His friend lay on the rocks below looking like a crumpled piece of paper.

No. This couldn't have happened. Not to Sampson. He's too careful.

The lifeless form lay stretched out on the rocks below, not moving. Conrad screamed Sampson's name again and again. No answer. Conrad's feet refused to move. His legs felt weak. He squatted, hoping a shorter drop would absorb the impact of him hitting the ground.

We've been friends since grade one. Sampson had always looked out for me. Made sure I looked both ways before crossing the street. Insisted I wear a helmet when bike riding. What do I do now?

IN THE END

Conrad looked at the five feet separating him from the entrance of the tunnel's crawl space.

Have to tell Perry.

His foot refused to move. He rolled on to his hands and knees. The surface's glue-grip hold broke. Piercing pain from rocks poking his knees foreshadowed an agonizing crawl back through the tunnel.

A minor suffering.

Nothing could compare to the loss of his father-figure friend, the one who had predicted trouble before it happened.

***

"What's wrong?" Perry pointed to Conrad's knee.

Conrad was unaware of grit imbedded in his knees and blood.

After mumbling his bombshell news, Conrad sank to the ground. Memories of him and Sampson washed over him. If it wasn't for Sampson, he'd never have learned to fish. He didn't like cleaning the fish, but Sampson ignored his objection. "I still don't like fishing," he mumbled.

"Afraid of the water. Can't swim." Conrad's feeble excuses had failed to convince Sampson. Sampson made him take swimming lessons until he reached junior lifesaver. Not complaining about the water ended Sampson's push for the next course.

If it wasn't for Sampson, I'd never have learned to ski. My "I might break my leg," objection hadn't work.

Instead, he coached me. Paid for my first ski trip. He said it was my birthday present.

I like skiing with the guys. And I will go on more ski trips with them even though Sampson won't be with me.

Conrad settled himself on the ground dimly aware of Perry calling for Arny. He didn't flinch as Perry used his T-shirt to clean the blood and grit from his knee. When the other guys returned, he sat by himself thinking of Sampson. He joined the rest of the boys for Perry's memorial service, but he couldn't share any stories of Sampson. His voice would crack.

CHAPTER 11

Loss

When is it reasonable for a person to pull out of the grip of grief? When can a person be expected to deal with reality? Answers for those questions troubled the boys before turning in for the night.

Their attempts to encourage Conrad to talk about Sampson, to join them in any small talk, failed. He sat looking at his shoes, saying nothing. When they quit trying to draw him into a conversation, he got up and sat by himself.

"I don't get it," whispered Brayden. "He wasn't that upset with Calvin's death or Jean's."

"Or Len and Larry's," said Terry in a voice loud enough for only Brayden and Graham to hear.

Silence settled over them.

"I guess he and Sampson were closer than we thought. Think he'll be able to deal with reality by tomorrow?" Terry's question hung unanswered.

Brayden looked across to Victor, Perry, and Arny huddled together whispering. *Wonder if they're figuring out what to do with Conrad.*

"What do you think?" Terry looked to Graham for a response.

Graham had been reviewing what he'd read about the stages of grief in his psychology class. The information didn't help. Everyone experienced loss and shock often differently.

Conrad's withdrawal seems like he is in the numbness stage. Like he doesn't want to experience anything in life. He doesn't want to feel hurt again. Better to protect yourself from life's pains. Graham shook his head. *But what do you do about it?*

He reviewed some of the next grief stages: denial, anger, scapegoating.

"Graham." Terry's louder call refocused Graham. "You okay?"

Graham nodded. "You were asking?"

"Any idea when you think he'll be feeling better?" asked Terry, nodding in Conrad's direction.

"Feeling normal," added Brayden.

"Hard to say." He looked around hoping to pass the question off to Victor. "I'd say that Conrad's in the early stages of grief. There are a number of stages." He listed a few. "I think we need to be prepared for bursts of anger. It may not happen either. He may jump all the way to temporarily dealing with reality like the rest of us."

"So, you're saying you don't know."

Graham nodded.

"I once had an aunt, strange person. She lost her husband. It took her years to recover. I think she was stuck in that numb stage," said Terry.

"That could be a problem for us tomorrow," said Brayden.

"Best wait 'til tomorrow," advised Graham. "Someone may have to sit with him while the rest of us hunt for a way out of here."

***

"Okay," said Conrad. The sound of his voice snapped him to the present. He reviewed what he just agreed to. The last words that came to him were Perry's. "Don't worry about mapping the tunnels. I'll do that when I return." Conrad remembered hearing that he would be staying with their gear.

Accepting his serving of pancakes from Perry, Conrad asked, "What's going on?"

Conrad learned Terry's flashlight died so he was going with Brayden to search the next tunnel on the right. Graham chose the second tunnel to the right. Victor volunteered to check the first tunnel to the left. Arny mentioned he had left three rocks at the entrance of a gentle sloping tunnel. He couldn't remember if it was the fourth or fifth tunnel to the right.

"But I'll find it," said Arny as he moved closer to Conrad. "I figure it's something my foot can handle now."

"Sounds like a fair walk. You sure you'll have no trouble going there and back?" As Perry spoke, he pointed to Arny's foot.

"You do what you must," Arny said with a grin. Victor had used the phrase earlier.

"What about you?" said Conrad, looking to Perry.

"I'm going to stay back and keep you company."

"Forget it. I'll be okay. Go and see if you can find a way out of here. That's more important."

Perry objected but Conrad insisted that he go. Perry said he'd check the third tunnel to the right.

Once he was alone, Conrad stared at the flickering lantern light. He'd turned it low to conserve fuel. Shortly, his thoughts turned to Sampson and his egg-seizing mission. *He was only being thoughtful, trying to give us a little variety in our diet. He didn't deserve to die.* Tears crept up again.

Conrad gave his head a shake and shifted his thoughts to Sampson's career ambitions. Sampson was looking at designing public buildings. At least all his drafting choices involved public buildings. His real passion was in interior design. "Giving buildings a personality," he said. His excitement caught people's attention. His focus on detail drew other's admiration.

"Now, we'll never know what he would have created," mumbled Conrad, shifting his position.

Conrad's thoughts drifted to a camping trip they had taken last year, a hiking adventure in the mountains two hours away from Sampson's home.

He and Sampson had broken away from the rest of the group and approached a small stream.

Something gripped Conrad's shoulder.

"Earth to Conrad," Perry said. Conrad opened his eyes and focused on Perry.

"Where were you?" asked Perry.

"The camping trip we took last year."

"Oh yeah. Good times." Perry glanced around. "Anybody else returned yet?"

Conrad shook his head. His drifting off prevented him from saying "not that I noticed."

Perry picked up his writing pad and began sketching what he found on his way to his tunnel. In answer to Conrad's question about what he found in his tunnel, he lied. "A dead end. Only fifty-two steps." Arny's tunnel wasn't recorded. Arny had walked past Perry looking for his downward-sloping tunnel.

"That felt good," said Perry. He put his pad down. In response to Conrad's furrowed forehead, he added, "Got to do something to occupy my mind otherwise I keep thinking of Sampson."

Conrad nodded. "Know what you mean."

Once again, Perry offered to keep Conrad company, but Conrad insisted that he continue the tunnel search. Perry told Conrad he'd join Victor. He needed to talk to a nonjudgmental person.

Perry found Victor's tunnel. It began ascending immediately. Its ascent allowed Perry to stand straight up and walk without the walls on either side, grabbing his clothes, but the beginning was short-lived. The tunnel veered sharply to the left. In his mind, that turn meant they were backtracking instead of progressing ahead. The tunnel's path became a climbing effort, short elevations to start with. Then Perry had to scramble up some portions. He found he had no time to think about Sampson. He had to search for footholds to continue.

Maybe I made a mistake coming after Victor.

He considered giving up when a fork appeared. His hope rose. The left direction resembled the original opening, a gentle ascent in a wide stand-up passage. Checking the ground for the rock clue, Perry found Victor had chosen the right, the challenging climbing option.

Like Sampson. Go right first, he thought.

Perry shook his head and picked his way up. This option was considerably narrower and lower. At times, he had to partially squat. Then he heard rocks tumbling. Perry stopped and listened. There it was again. Rocks, small ones.

Victor? he wondered.

He waited. A lantern light appeared above him, then Victor's runners. Perry aimed his flashlight beam up so that Victor would know someone was waiting for him.

"Perry! What are you doing here? Anything wrong?"

"No. Just thought I would come and join you." Perry began working his way down the tunnel. "Nothing at the end of your tunnel?"

"A dead end."

Perry's foot missed its grip, and he slid two feet. He tore a hole in his pants. Blood oozed from his knee.

"You okay?"

"Yeah, just didn't pay attention to what I was doing." Perry continued down the tunnel with more care until he reached the fork.

Victor asked him to adjust the signal rocks to indicate that they were going to the left. As Perry followed Victor's instructions, Victor said, "You must have found the end in your tunnel pretty fast. Anything interesting?"

Perry started up the left fork, then waited for Victor. When he could see him, he said, "I feel like I'm losing it."

"What?"

"This place gave me the creeps." Perry studied his friend's face. No judgement.

"Because—"

"Can I be completely honest with you?"

"Certainly."

No hesitation. What Perry hoped for. Still studying Victor's face, Perry said, "Do you ever get the feeling that someone is watching you? Someone like a pickpocket who's looking for a chance to steal your camera or wallet?"

"Can't say as I have."

"Well, that's the experience that I had descending into that dark tunnel. I'm sure I detected a faint stinky smell, like a guy sweating. Felt like someone was behind me, just out of my sight. *That* I handled but then there was a drowsy feeling. I felt warm, really relaxed. I couldn't stop yawning. It took an effort to move my hands. That scared me. Crazy! I backed out as fast as I could. It took a while before I felt like my head was screwed on properly."

Victor's brow furrowed. "Can't say I've had that experience."

"So far, in this tunnel I haven't either."

"Do you have that feeling in the main tunnel?"

"At times, like I'm being watched? Yes. No smell, but the feeling that someone is about to cause harm of some sort. It's worse in these side tunnels. It's like the devil is prowling around here waiting for me to make a mistake. Waiting to snatch me."

"I see why you feel like you're losing it."

"Exactly! You don't think I'm crazy, do you?"

Victor searched for a nonthreatening response. "No, but I wouldn't be telling the other guys. Some might not understand that you may have a sixth sense in play here."

"What do you think our chances are of us getting out of here, of exploring outside paths?" asked Perry.

"Right now, I think we're stuck with poking around in here. As the oil for our lanterns gives out and flashlights die, we'll be forced to reconsider our goals."

"Well, right now, Arny and I are the only ones with flashlights. Conrad told me he has one last battery. For which flashlight, I don't know. I wonder how long our lanterns will hold out."

IN THE END

"I figure when we start to use the last battery, we'll make daylight a priority. The last thing I want to do is feel my way around these tunnels." Victor slowly shook his head to emphasize his position.

Perry noted a light breeze. *Third time. Opening ahead. Maybe a way out.* He took Victor's lantern, turned his flashlight off, and handed it to Victor. Together they walked along a gentle upward sloping passageway. Their search ended when they approached a cave-in. Only a small hole to the outside remained.

The hour that it took to work their way back to the main tunnel gave Victor a chance to talk about memories of Sampson that kept replaying in his head. He was glad to hear that Perry too couldn't take his mind off their fallen friend.

After entering the main tunnel, Victor suggested that Perry should stay with their supplies and focus on recording the searches. When Victor and Perry found Conrad, he was dozing in the dim light. He would ask Conrad to join him on his next tunnel search.

"Anybody returned yet?" asked Perry.

After shaking off his drowsiness, Conrad said, "Graham. He left to check on whatever tunnel came up next. His tunnel ended with some kind of falling water or stream. He wasn't too clear." Conrad struggled to his feet.

As Conrad was yawning, Brayden and Terry approached. "Nothing of importance in our tunnel," said Brayden.

Brayden walked to a sleeping bag. He rolled it out and said he wanted a little rest before continuing on.

"Good idea," said Terry. He grabbed a soft backpack to use for a pillow and rolled out his sleeping bag.

"What time is it?" asked Conrad, stretching.

Checking his watch Terry said, "10:20."

"I've had my sleep. I'm going to do some searching myself." Conrad looked at Perry. "You can be point person again. Okay? It's just too boring sitting here."

Perry nodded.

"Good idea," said Victor, moving toward Conrad. "I'll come with you."

Conrad whipped around and faced Victor. "I said *I* will do some searching." His voice was two octaves higher than necessary. "I don't need someone to babysit me." Without waiting for a response, he picked up Victor's flashlight and marched down the main tunnel.

After a while, Conrad found the circle of rocks with a bar in the middle before the first tunnel to the right, the one Brayden and Terry had checked. Then he saw the same indicator before Graham's tunnel. When he found Perry's tunnel, he saw the rocks indicating he had gone in.

No six-rock indicator saying not to go in!

He came to Victor's tunnel to the left and then Graham's to the right. Continuing on, he came to a six-foot-wide space with three entrances. The one to his left was marked with six stones.

A gentle incline. Where Arny is, I'll bet. Hope he's okay.

Looking straight ahead, he guessed that was the path that Sampson had led them down.

Next day, we should move our belongings to this spot, thought Conrad.

Conrad placed the six-stone marker indicating he went to his right. As he had walked down the tunnel, his thoughts turned to Calvin.

So happy-go-lucky. He introduced me to Susan. Never thanked him.

His daydreaming stopped. He frowned. A little way in, the six-foot-high tunnel shrank to four feet. *Going to have a sore back.* He shook his head. *Never know what these passages will present.* Sharp turns and drops forced him to focus where he placed his feet.

CHAPTER 12

At Peace

When Arny began to search for his tunnel, he hadn't realized how far away it was from their last camping spot or how many branch tunnels there were. While he thought his small pile of rocks would identify the tunnel that he wanted to explore, it wasn't the rocks that clued him in. It was the tunnel's large area with a four-way intersection. He remembered when Sampson had been forced with a choice of going straight, right or left. Arny felt a soft breeze to his right. After Sampson had decided to go straight, Arny had left some of his rocks in the tunnel entrance to his right.

Now, what to do? Arny shone the flashlight farther down the main tunnel that he'd been following. Nothing new. He looked back from where he had come. There was no sign of his friends. He felt a slight breeze, now to his left.

Same breeze calling me, he thought. Seeing the tunnel's gentle downward slope, he expected an easy walk. *No slouching.* He began his exploring. Before long, he encountered two long narrow rock piles.

Dead miners, he guessed as he walked by them.

He found eight smaller branch tunnels, almost all shorter requiring him to crawl if he chose to enter them. Those he ignored, as he did when he saw two more miners' graves. He strolled through his chosen tunnel, sometimes veering to the right and sometimes to the left, but always going down. Its slope gradually became steeper, forcing him to take shorter steps.

Then came the sound of falling water. Without realizing it, he quickened his pace. And there was something in the air. His first guess, the refreshing smell of moisture after a rainfall. But there was more. It was pleasant, begging him to slowly inhale more deeply.

The last time he stopped what he was doing to savor an enticing scent was when he hugged Trish after coming home from a baseball game with the guys. Instead of hanging up his sweater as he usually did, he held on to Trish, enjoying the smell of her washed hair. "New shampoo," she said, "Apple blossom."

When they were watching TV following supper, he'd edged closer to her. He had to smell her hair again. *Maybe too close.* Twice she moved away.

How nice it would be if Trish were here.

Arny imagined drawing up closer to her, even closer if he could.

Feels warm.

He unbuttoned a couple of buttons on his shirt, then all of them.

Would that worry her?

He stretched his arm out as if to put it around her shoulder. A cool, damp sensation touched his hand. He pulled his arm back.

What happened?

Looking around, he could only see the tunnel wall within his reach. A slight dizziness. He reached out to steady himself. The moment he touched the wall, he knew where that earlier cool dampness came from. Confused, he stood trying to make sense of what had just happened.

There it is again.

He heard the sound of falling water. His flashlight poked into the darkness ahead, but he saw nothing.

How is that possible? I don't see anything.

The sound beckoned him. Come. He redirected the light to the path right before his feet. Slowly sliding one foot in front of the other, he moved ahead. The slope was steep. In the midst of the darkness, encouragement came from the sound of the waterfall. Louder. Closer. The air became moister. The temperature rose. He fanned himself with his hand. It didn't help.

Then the footpath disappeared. His probing light discovered a chasm, a deep drop he guessed. Waves gently slapped the rocky side.

Who turned up the heat?

No breeze. His light beam poked around in the darkness. He forced his eyes to search the dark expanse. For what he wasn't sure. Then, across the chasm, he saw a flickering light.

A campfire?

The more he looked at the light, the more he became convinced he was seeing a small fire. Movement in the glow of fire surprised him. He redirected the flashlight beam. There was something there. He was sure of it. In dim light, a girl's head appeared. Auburn ringlets dropped to her shoulder. She looked at the ground. Seconds later, she looked up as if to confirm she still had Arny's attention.

Then Arny sensed, not heard her call out. "Hi."

Hesitantly, Arny responded, "Hi." The sound of his voice echoed off the rocks.

Again, he sensed, not saw her smile. A glowing smile, a smile he'd seen before, a smile he'd seen from Trish when he showed up for their date.

I'm not alone.

The girl bent down and placed some sticks in the fire. When she stood up, she looked in his direction. A telepathic message—"May I help you?"

Arny stood confused. He stared at the girl as she ran her fingers through her hair and looked away. "Come over here," he wanted to say to the apparition.

She took a couple of steps away from him, farther from the campfire light.

Arny's immediate reaction was, "No. Don't go. Wait." A reaction he once had when he refused to explain to Trish why he had showed up an hour late. She'd turned to walk away.

As if the girl with the auburn hair heard his words, she stopped then slowly looked up at him.

A wave of heat engulfed Arny. Embarrassed for exposing his feelings of wanting to be with her, he looked away. A flash of anger bit him.

Why did he break the visual line of communication with this beautiful girl? Why was he ruining any chance of being with the girl who looked a bit like Trish?

Seconds later, he sensed her say, "Come here." He imagined standing inches away from her. A playful smile appeared followed by "Come closer."

"Yes," said Arny, anxious to meet his dear friend. He set the flashlight down and dived into the lake below. It took only a couple of minutes to swim to the other side of the chasm. Attempts to scale the rock face failed the first time. Wet hands and wet feet found no lasting grip. He tried a second time, a third time, a fourth time, a ...

***

Victor watched Conrad disappear into the darkness. *All I said was "I'll come with you." Just thought he'd like a little company. Why couldn't Conrad see I was trying to be a good friend?* thought Victor. Victor sat down. He shook his head, still baffled about how his good intention backfired.

After a while, Graham sat beside Victor. "You know that wasn't your fault," he said. Responding to Victor's puzzled look, he added, "Conrad's reaction. He's still grieving."

"Yeah, I figured that. I think it's a bad idea for any of us to be alone. At a time like this, we should have someone to talk to."

"So, what do we do now?"

"I'd like to get back to checking these tunnels, but if I leave now, I might run into Conrad. Don't want him to think I'm checking up on him."

"Then I may have a solution."

Victor looked at Graham surprised.

"Perry and I were talking. We can't figure out what's happened to Arny. Perry isn't too concerned. He guessed Arny told Conrad where he was going, but Arny's been gone a long time.

"You're right. I should find him." Victor stood up, relieved he had good reason to go down the tunnel. "Wanna come?" he asked, looking at Graham.

"You bet."

Perry asked if he could come too. Brayden and Terry followed suit. Conrad's considerable head start meant there was no chance of them bumping into him while he was angry. Once they reached the four-way intersection, they had a problem. Which way did Arny go? The rock indicators showed one person went right and another went left.

"We could wait here until either Arny or Conrad shows up," suggested Perry.

Because the opening at this intersection was much larger than the tunnel path, Victor suggested they move their supplies to this new location. Brayden, Graham, and Terry agreed. Perry volunteered to wait for Arny or Conrad to show up.

Conrad returned first, and he was anxious to tell of his findings. As he talked, Perry sketched his information on a new sheet of paper.

"Nine branches! Can you believe that?" began Conrad. "Most were stubby buggers, short crawl spaces. Like the mystery men only dug ten, fifteen feet and then quit. There was one different tunnel. It dropped sharply, like going down a ladder into a basement. At the bottom, I found a large empty room. If it was easy to get to, I would have thought that was a main storage area or even sleeping quarters."

Then Victor, Brayden, Graham, and Terry showed up with supplies tightly strapped to their bodies and both arms loaded. Exhausted, they dropped their load, sat down, and took a deep drink. Then they listened to Conrad retell his exploring story. When he finished, they sat in silence. Perry's head was bowed. Terry asked him if he was tired.

"No. I was praying. Dad said when times are really tough, ask God for strength and wisdom."

"I was thinking of my father too," added Graham. "If I was home, I expect we'd be going golfing."

Brayden and Victor admitted their thoughts were with their families too. Silence returned. Thoughts focused on family.

IN THE END

After a while, Victor broke the silence. "What do you say we start searching for Arny?"

He received overwhelming support. Perry looked at the tunnel that Arny had gone down. Dark. Sloping down. He offered to stay behind and organize their camping gear.

Victor remembered Perry's experience in the last tunnel. Before the other boys could say anything, Victor said, "Good idea."

The four boys started down the tunnel each carrying a lantern. They followed Victor. As they encountered branch tunnels, one of the boys would go into it. Arny might not have had enough rocks to indicate the direction he took.

Conrad volunteered first. He had to crouch a little, but he suspected others might require crawling. He was right. Terry and Graham had to squat. Brayden's required him to move on his belly.

Victor memorized who went down each side tunnel. Several times he called out for Arny. No answer. By the time that Victor reached the fourth tunnel, Conrad had caught up to him. His tunnel was short. Victor planned to search this passageway, but Conrad stepped ahead of him. At the next branch, Victor waited for someone to catch up to him. Someone had to be in the main tunnel in case Arny came walking back.

This is taking a long time. Where could he have gotten to?

Feeling a little unsteady, Victor sat down. His thoughts drifted to the fun he and Arny shared on ski trips, camping outings, and attending football and soccer matches. In the middle of his recollections, he caught himself thinking of Arny in the past.

Think of Arny in the present. He isn't dead you idiot.

With his reprimand in mind, he turned his attention to plans he and Arny had made for the rest of the summer—canoeing and fishing in Emerald Lake National Park and joining the archery club in the September. How Arny got him to volunteer to help Mr. Oms, Arny's uncle, with his potato harvest, Victor didn't know. *Sometimes he has a way of sucking me in.*

When Graham and Terry returned, Graham asked, "You okay?"

"Yeah. Just needed a little rest." As soon as Victor stood up, Brayden went into the side tunnel. Terry and Victor advanced down the tunnel that they thought Arny had used. Victor noticed their path was steeper. He felt a slight breeze. Then came to another branch tunnel. Terry stepped into it.

When Victor reached the next branch passageway, he felt unsteady on his feet. He sat down and partly unbuttoned his shirt. Then he heard the sound of falling water. The air felt moist.

Getting close?

He wanted to investigate what was ahead, but he knew he couldn't take a chance that Arny might come crawling out of the passageway to his right. When Conrad showed up again, Victor began to wonder what happened to Brayden.

Brayden went up the third tunnel, I think. Must remember that.

Once Conrad stepped into the tunnel, Victor walked ahead to investigate the sound of the waterfall and to investigate where a soft breeze was coming from. He found Arny's flashlight sitting on the ground, dimly pointing out into the darkness. He shook his head.

Strange.

His light poked around the ground searching for Arny. He found a black void, then the edge of the crevice. Waves slapping rocks. He shone his light down to see it reflect off water. The beam scouted the lake's surface below. Nothing. Victor adopted a grid search pattern on the surface of the lake. He scoured about two-thirds of the lake's surface.

Something floating?

He narrowed the beam for greater light intensity.

No doubt. Arny. Floating.

He shut the light off and stared into the darkness where he saw his friend's body. The vision revealed by the light remained burned into his mind.

After a while, he whispered. "I'm sorry, I never told you how much I admired your positive nature, your easy-going spirit. Many times, I wished I could be more like you." With tears in his eyes, he added, "Goodbye, good friend." He stood, petrified until Graham tapped him on the shoulder.

"Victor?"

After hearing his name, a second time Victor pointed into the darkness below. "Arny," he said.

Looking at Victor's partially opened shirt, Graham wondered, *Could he be hallucinating?* "You sure?" he asked.

With blurry eyes, Victor looked on the ground. His light pointed to Arny's almost dead flashlight. "He left that." Victor sank to the ground.

In the light of Graham's lantern, both boys stared into the emptiness until Terry and Conrad arrived. They guessed what had arrested their friends. Conrad, who was the last to arrive, offered to get Perry so that he could lead a memorial service.

Graham's no stopped him. Before Conrad could question him, Graham walked up to Conrad. He whispered, "Look at Victor."

Conrad said nothing.

"Feel hot?"

Conrad shook his head.

Pointing to Victor's open shirt, Graham said, "He seems to feel hot."

Conrad stared at Victor who was looking intently at the ground.

"This isn't the first time he's had to sit down either. I'm guessing he's feeling a little dizzy."

Conrad's eyes widened. Remembering his experience in the tunnel where Len and Larry died, he said, "Gas?"

"I think so."

"But the rest of us—"

"Haven't been in this part of the tunnel for a long time. He has."

"Then we've got to get out of here," said Conrad.

Graham nodded. "Let's help him up."

Graham and Conrad took turns walking with Victor. By the time they reached the campsite where Perry was, Victor was able to walk on his own. Graham broke the news of Arny's death.

Shaking his head, Perry said, "I was afraid something like that had happened. He was gone too long."

"I'll miss his happy-go-lucky spirit," said Conrad. "He was too good a guy to die."

"He was, but he'll be fine now. He's in heaven. He's at peace, like Sampson."

Perry's religious references used to irk Conrad. They seemed unreal.

Phony. Not how I would see life.

Sampson had quelled Conrad's skepticism. He told Conrad that Perry was no weirder than Conrad who had frequently peppered his remarks with hockey comparisons—when making a shot in darts or pool Conrad often crowed, "He shoots. He scores." In card games when his opponent won, Conrad often said, "Next hand we crash 'em into the boards." After that revelation, Conrad weeded out his hockey language.

Now Perry's words, "He's at peace," comforted Conrad. Half-speaking to himself and half to Perry, he said, "I wish I was there."

Perry looked at his friend. "We'll get through this. We will." He put a hand on Conrad's shoulder. Conrad nodded.

The boys formed a tight circle. Three lanterns glowed softly. They first focused on Arny. When it came time for their prayer, Perry began by pouring out his heart, touching on the feelings of loss he'd just heard. He asked for the Lord's comfort. It was a longer prayer than usual. As before, he ended with the boys reciting the Lord's Prayer. To him, it affirmed they were one body.

When the boys broke up to sit by themselves, Conrad nudged Perry to the side. In a low voice, he said, "You sound like you really think Arny is at peace."

"I do. I believe he's in heaven. You know, no pain. No sickness. No stress." Conrad's focused attention encouraged Perry to continue. "You know, I wouldn't be surprised if he's looking down on us, feeling sorry for us. He might be talking and laughing with Larry and Len and Sampson."

"And Calvin and Jean?"

"Right," said Perry.

"That would be nice. I'd like to believe that."

"Then do. I'll pray for you."

"Thanks." With a slight smile, Conrad looked for a place to lie down. Like the others, he then crawled into his sleeping bag, where he could think about their predicament and about what Perry had said.

CHAPTER 13

A Way Out

Perry's circadian rhythm woke him up before everyone else. His sense of responsibility motivated him to make breakfast. The other boys woke up to sounds of cooking. Lanterns were turned on. Some thanked Perry for working on breakfast. No one complained about the same food. They were hungry, very hungry.

Morning conversation changed the day's goals. Instead of checking the tunnels, they decided to find a way out of the underground labyrinth. As soon as the meal was finished in a business manner, everyone headed down the main tunnel, the one that Sampson had originally used.

With the appearance of the next four openings, Graham, Brayden, Victor, and Terry each chose to check a passageway angling down and to the right. None were wide or tall. These secondary choices suggested little use, little value, but they had to be checked to be certain they held no escape route.

Perry chose to go with Conrad. He felt safer than going up a tunnel himself. They held out for a tunnel angling up and were rewarded. It went left, was wider and taller than other branches. The slight upward grade offered no walking challenge. Gentle turns enabled them to gaze ahead to the full extent of their lantern's light. No need to worry about surprises. He began counting his steps to record on his map.

They passed two piles of rocks covering mystery men bodies. Two shovels lay on top marking the men's grave. Guessing that a cave-in had caught the men, the two boys shone their lanterns along the walls and ceiling to check for signs of a structural failure. They saw none. Feeling a little safer, they slowly continued.

Perry returned to counting steps. Three hundred and twenty paces took them to a divide. The tunnel to the left was a little narrower and shorter than the one they were in but larger than the tunnels that their friends had taken. Conrad, a head taller than Perry, waited for his friend to volunteer to check the left tunnel.

"We could continue together to check this main branch out," said Perry. He looked down their main tunnel hoping to see something that would send them both to investigate.

"Or you could catch up with up me when you're finished checking this tunnel." Conrad pointed to the tunnel to his left. "I don't expect you'll miss anything worthwhile. I'll bet you even come up with something more interesting than I do."

Perry remained unimpressed.

"I'll go slowly so you won't have that far to go to catch up."

"And I'd do the same for you."

"Then it is agreed that we should split up, cover more area faster?"

"Agreed," said Perry, knowing Conrad's decision. "But you owe me." He bent a little and stepped into the left-heading tunnel. Conrad watched his friend carefully placing his feet on the uneven ground.

When Perry walked beyond the range of Conrad's lantern's light, Conrad leisurely strolled down his tunnel. His thoughts drifted to the last time Perry had said, "You owe me."

It was late at Conrad's birthday party. Perry, Terry, and Victor had stayed behind to play poker with Conrad. Conrad was considered a very good player but that night he'd lost heavily. His frustration delighted an intoxicated Terry. Victor had taken a shot at Conrad's ego—*Some card shark you are,* he said. Terry's insanely loud laughter drove Conrad crazy, but he couldn't deny the truth. He was a loser. Then Perry, who had been low-key about Conrad's losses, followed Conrad to the washroom. Before Conrad closed the door, Perry pushed himself in.

"I can tell you why you have such a bad streak of luck," Perry began, "but you have to promise me that what I tell you, you will keep a secret."

After Conrad promised, Perry told him how Conrad's strong bidding hands prompted Lizzy, Terry's girlfriend, to look over Conrad's shoulder to see if he was bluffing. Then, while still behind Conrad's back, she would signal Terry.

In answer to Conrad's shocked plea—why—Perry said, "Terry's second present for you—experience a little humility. *Broaden your character.* "They're only out to have a little fun with you." Perry had added, "Let them think they've succeeded. After all, we're only playing with Monopoly money."

At first, Conrad had wanted to spoil their little lark, but Perry convinced him to let it go.

"You owe me," said Perry.

Sunshine reflected from the sides of the tunnel. Conrad redirected his focus. He blew the light out of his lantern and looked back. No sign of Perry. He quickened his pace. A small tunnel branched off to his right. He ignored it. The increased temperature drew him on. After a few minutes, he found himself standing on a very wide ledge bathed in sun.

A mini oven, he thought.

The ledge stretched out for at least one hundred feet. After walking across two-thirds of the open area, Conrad discovered a break in the ledge. A two-hundred-foot drop divided the sunbaked flat surface.

Like an earthquake had split the surface in two.

He estimated the divide between the two ledges to be about five feet.

Not impossible to cross.

In grade twelve, he'd entered in the track meet as a broad jumper. He'd almost made six feet, not enough to win anything, but it was one of his best jumps.

IN THE END

Conrad's gaze shifted to the blue sky and then in the distance to the rainbow bending behind the folded rocks ahead of him.

Missed a rainfall.

At the end of the multicolor arc, a light flashed infrequently. It came from below and behind the rocks. Curious, Conrad walked along the narrowing ledge. Each step he took revealed a similar ledge on the opposite side of the divide and then a steep gravel slope dropping like a ski hill to the floor of the valley.

A butt-slide to the bottom. It's possible.

Continuing along the now two-foot wide ledge that turned sharply into the divide, Conrad saw the source of the flashing light. The sun's rays reflected off a two-tiered waterfall that dropped to a lake on the valley floor.

Looking again at the graveled slope, he imagined jabbing a shovel into the gravel to slow the descent to the bottom.

Then a half-mile walk to the lake. We'd be out of the tunnels. It can be done.

His eyes followed his curving ledge. It continued to narrow to a foot wide. At the far end it was only about three feet away from the opposite ledge.

Too narrow a path to get a good running start to make the jump. But one could throw supplies across the divide from there.

Conrad retraced his steps until he was at the broadest part of the ledge. He walked up to a boulder partly encased in the rock face. Bending his back into the boulder's curved face, he felt the sunbaked shirt burn into his stomach and a similar sensation on the pant legs. He closed his eyes and imagined being on a beach tanning. Minutes drifted by before the image of the lake below and the gravel slope demanded his attention.

Sliding down. No big deal. Fresh water. Camping at the lake. A safe base from which to explore. Better than poking around in the darkness. It's like a pot of gold at the end of the rainbow. All one needs to do is cross this five-foot divide.

Cross it. Jump across it. Could it be done? I could. I've jumped that distance before.

To prove he could do it, he picked up a couple of rocks and paced out six feet. One rock was placed at either end of his jumping area. His first running jump covered almost four feet.

Need a serious run.

A second effort increased his jumping distance to a little over five feet. Six more tries brought him close to the six feet. He added several tears to his knees and one on his butt when he fell backward. Thinking that he needed a longer run, he moved his stone markers farther along the ledge. He was about to make a second attempt to race to his new jumping off point when Perry appeared.

"Having fun?" asked Perry after walking up to a heavy breathing Conrad.

"Watch this."

Conrad ran as fast as he could and jumped. He checked his distance.

"More than six feet. Good."

He led Perry to the point where they could both see the gravel slope and a part of the lake on the valley floor. Then he explained he was going to jump across the divide to check out the path to the gravel slope.

"This is the answer we've been looking for. No more poking around in dead-end tunnels," he said, hoping Perry would catch his excitement.

"Too dangerous." Perry shook his head.

"What do you mean too dangerous? Just watch this." He returned to his starting point for another run. When Perry called out to object, Conrad waved his objection away with "Just watch this." He ran faster than ever, intent on increasing his jumping distance. He succeeded. His jumping distance increased by six inches.

"That's more than enough."

Again, Perry walked up to the panting Conrad. "You don't get it. I'm not jumping to my death."

Walking to his starting point, Conrad said, "Don't be such a pessimist. You can do it." He looked back to see that Perry hadn't moved. "Come on. Give it a try."

"Fine. Don't believe me. You'll see."

Perry's run landed him about three feet. Conrad dismissed his first effort as just that, a first effort. He pointed out that he'd only jumped four feet on his first try. When Perry's second effort produced the same result, Conrad said, "This time run like you have a black bear running after you." Perry's third jump increased by five inches.

"With practice, you'll get better," insisted Conrad. Perry repeated his decision not to jump the divide. "You mean if the rest of the group decides to make the jump, you will stay here by yourself? Don't be such a chicken."

The prospect frightened Perry. He knew he couldn't make the jump. Attempting to sound certain, he said, "They won't."

"We'll see. I suggest you practice your jumping like I did. In the meantime, I'm going to jump the divide. I want to see what the passageway to that slope is like, see if the slope can be reached easily."

Perry was tempted to convince Conrad to abandon his plan, but Conrad was already lining up for his jump. He watched, praying that Conrad would make it over safely. Conrad's victory shout proclaimed his success.

Conrad poked his head down a tunnel. Then he walked to the far end of the ledge.

"Hey," he shouted. "It's an easy slide down." For a while, he stood admiring the water falling and the lake below. He saw a stream pulling away from the lake and winding around the far rock bed. Upon returning to the ledge near Perry, he said, "There's beautiful lake down there. You have to see it."

"Yeah."

From Perry's lack of enthusiasm, Conrad knew Perry wouldn't attempt the jump. Probably wouldn't try to convince the rest of the guys to see that this was their best chance to get out of the dark tunnels.

"Okay. I'm coming back," he shouted.

IN THE END

Conrad had a shorter running distance for his jump, but it didn't bother him. He went to the far end of the ledge and charged to the divide. He knew he could make the jump. His foot slipped on some loose sand as he launched himself into the air. It cost him more than a foot in his sailing distance. He was too far away from ledge to grab it.

Perry watched Conrad's torso then his terrified face disappeared. Conrad's "No-o-o" echoed off the walls of the divide. There was silence. Perry stood in the heat of the sun's rays replaying the jump, imagining Conrad making it. But his eyes told him it wasn't real.

Anchored to the spot where he last saw Conrad, he thought of the fun they had. He could be so driven. The last time he'd seen Conrad so driven was when he was asked to be the fourth in a Texas scramble golf tournament. The course pro was on his team. Perry shook his head thinking, *No more.*

Perry dragged his feet on the way to the main tunnel. He didn't want to tell his friends about Conrad's death.

It made no sense. Conrad shouldn't have died. He wasn't alone like Arny or Jean or Calvin. Conrad wasn't in the dark where some mysterious force corrupted his mind. No. He shouldn't have died.

A protruding rock in the middle of the tunnel's path caused Perry to stumble. His shoulder bounced off the side of the tunnel. Pain shot up his right arm felt like someone slugged him.

I won't tell them everything. How many times he practiced the jump, that he made the jump once, about the gravel slope and lake beyond the far ledge, the other tunnel across the divide. Just say he failed to jump far enough to reach the far side. Really that's all they need to know.

Perry's thoughts returned to his practice jumps—*three feet, three feet, almost four feet. Knew I couldn't do it. Good I didn't try. Conrad shouldn't have tried either. He seemed so certain. Sure, he cleared six feet after about a dozen tries. A foot extra. Not much of a safety margin. I should have stopped him.*

Reviewing the mishap grew a throbbing pain in the back of Perry's head. The pain reached around to the back of his neck. The grip, gentle, gradually increased with the promise of being unrelenting.

Perry reached their camp site. The others had returned.

Graham called, "Hey, Perry." When Perry didn't respond, Graham said, "Why so glum? Where's Conrad?"

"You back already?" mumbled Perry.

"Yeah. I explored two tunnels during your absence. Granted they were short, but it's two less we have to do." Seeing Perry's drooping face and his barely audible response, he guessed Perry had something he wasn't anxious to share. "Where's Conrad?"

"Conrad's dead."

"What!" Terry jumped to his feet.

"Conrad was jumping over a divide and didn't make it."

Graham and Terry stood in shock.

"I couldn't reach him. I rushed to the edge of the ledge, but he'd fallen too far." Perry shook his head. "I wasn't close enough to grab his hand."

"Lucky for you that you didn't grab him. He'd have pulled you down with him," said Victor.

The prospect that he missed being pulled down with Conrad eased his guilt.

Terry suggested they go to the site where Perry last saw Conrad, but Perry told them there was nothing to see. His body was almost out of sight at the bottom of the divide. His insistence succeeded in convincing them to hold a quiet memorial for Conrad where they were.

As usual, they shared their favorite memories of Conrad. After a while, Perry led in prayer. Together they said the Lord's Prayer and remained sitting in a circle. They silently stared at the ground. Each remembered other special times with Conrad.

"Guys, I've got to say this." Brayden statement was low, but loud enough for the others to hear. Brayden looked around. When everyone was facing him, he added, "I'm really sick of this place."

Terry agreed saying, "We're being picked off one by one. By whom or what I don't know. It's not fair. We've done nothing wrong."

"We should just walk straight out of here. No more checking these useless tunnels. They're all dead ends or death traps." Brayden looked to see who would challenge him.

Standing up too, Graham said, "I'm all for that."

"It's possible," said Victor. "I now believe I know our way back to our starting point."

"Good," said Perry. "That's what I wanted to hear. How long do you think it will take?"

"Don't really know," said Victor. "It's not too close, but I'm sure I can find it from here."

"Let's do it." Terry stood up, picked up a backpack, his sleeping bag, and a lantern. "I'm ready." He grabbed the coiled rope that he'd been carrying.

"Wait a minute," said Victor standing up. "Terry, what time is it?"

Checking his watch, Terry answered, "7:42."

"Then I suggest we get a good night's sleep and start first thing tomorrow morning. Like I said, I'm not sure how far we have to go. I'd like to arrive in the daylight." He took the rope and the sleeping bag from his friend.

"Ah-h-h-h. Guys."

Perry's hesitant interruption caught them by surprise. The coiled rope had given Perry an idea. An idea that would get them out of the tunnels after an hour's walk. An idea that could get them camping by a lake in only a few hours.

"You're in pretty good shape, aren't you?" Perry nodded first to Victor and then to Terry. They both confirmed his impression.

"I'm going to suggest something that is a little dangerous, but if it works, tomorrow we won't have to wait very long to have the sun on our backs. We may be at the back door of Vanna too."

Having captured their attention, he told them about Conrad's efforts and initial success in jumping over the divide. He confessed that he'd never be able to do it. He said, "But if we go to the narrowest part of the divide—" looking at Terry he said, "and you're on the other side, you could throw one end of the rope to me. I'd then swing over to your side and you could pull me up."

"Or you could climb up."

"Maybe." Looking at Graham, Perry said, "We could do it. Really." Seeing Brayden shake his head at the prospect, he added, "You could too, Bray. If I could, I know you could."

"Anything to get out of here sooner. This place is giving me the creeps." Terry looked at Victor. "You willing to check it out?" Victor nodded. "Nothing to lose." Terry directed the same question first to Graham and then Brayden. Peer pressure secured Brayden's support.

"Then it's agreed," said Victor. "First thing next day we'll check Perry's idea out."

"Hey, Perry. Why don't you read some more of what the mystery men wrote about Vanna? Give us something even more positive to look forward to." Terry looked to the others. They nodded.

Perry hunted around in the mystery men's journals until he found what he was looking for. He began with a haiku that he was sure they would relate to.

>Deep in a dark mine
>Remember Vanna

My prime life-line hope.

Then he read a few other haikus.

> Fishing, canoeing
> Paddleboats and water-skis
> My water-fun home

> Bikes, scooters, mopeds
> Cycling routes and walking lanes
> Playful wandering.

> One large family.
> Everyone knows everyone.
> Close community.

And because Graham had been active in the high school's drama club, he read;

> Drama festivals
> Flourishing art galleries
> Passion lover's home.

For a short time, they expressed hopes of what they might find in Vanna. Then they crawled into their sleeping bags.

Victor's head rested on his packed backpack. No pillow but it offered enough support. Images of fishing, canoeing, and riding a bike in a park played in his head.

Vanna, a holiday resort.

IN THE END

The image coupled with his man cave friends laughing and horsing around.

No. No Arny. No Calvin. No Jean. No Len. No Conrad.

The desire to tan on a beach disappeared. His analytical mind pushed away the creeping desire to sleep. He couldn't stop thinking about Conrad.

Conrad shouldn't have failed to make his jump. It's not like him.

He thought of the time he convinced Conrad to go to Jasper to ski for the weekend. At first Conrad resisted. He'd never gone. He thought he wasn't good enough. Victor described the evening fun he'd miss—sitting before a roaring fire, drinking and playing Risk or Monopoly or canasta with the guys. Conrad hung on to the fear that he'd break an arm or leg and be stuck in the hospital.

Was it my offer to pay the first day's lift ticket or my suggestion that he take a brush-up lesson on skiing that convinced him?

Conrad came, and he had fun. The event reminded Victor that Conrad always expected the worst. He'd do whatever it took to prevent something ruining a good time. Then Victor recalled Perry's description of Conrad practicing.

Just like Conrad. Before doing his jump, he'd have practiced, made sure he could clear the distance. He'd have made sure he was confident of making the jump first. Confidence! That's it. On his first jump, he was probably afraid he wouldn't make it. He'd put every-

thing into his leap. On the return jump he was confident, over-confident. He didn't try as hard. That's it.

Victor took a deep breath. He solved the dilemma. He knew what caused Conrad's death. He knew what to avoid tomorrow.

CHAPTER 14

A Leap of Faith

With breakfast finished and cooking supplies packed, Perry and Victor walked out to the ledge where Conrad had died. Perry set a faster pace than the other boys so he and Victor would have a private space. He had glanced back over his shoulder several times.

"Second thoughts?" Victor's brow furrowed.

Perry glanced back again. Everyone else was preoccupied. In a lowered tone, Perry said, "We have to get out of here as soon as possible." He offered nothing more.

Victor waited a bit then said, "We are. Why the concern?"

"You won't laugh at me or think I'm losing it?"

Victor shook his head and walked a little closer to his friend.

Looking straight ahead, Perry began, "Last night, I couldn't shake the feeling that we have been walking around in the devil's home. He was furious with us, and he planned to claim more of us before we left."

"A premonition?"

"Felt like it. I couldn't fall asleep for hours. It was like I was trying to stay awake. I intended to catch him attempting to claim another of his trespassing bodies. I know this is stupid, but the first thing I did when I woke up was check to see that we were all still alive."

Victor said nothing until after they'd traveled more than a hundred paces. "Are you nervous about us crossing that divide?"

Perry's brief glance confirmed what Victor suspected.

"Would you feel safer if I was the first person to swing across the divide and handle the rope?" In response to Perry's smile, Victor put an arm on Perry's shoulder and said, "Consider it done."

The morning's bright sun did little to welcome Perry when they arrived at the ominous ledge. Like yesterday, there was no breeze. The area was cooler. The surrounding rocks hadn't warmed to reflect the heat. The gap by the ledge looked every bit as threatening as it did earlier.

Once more, Perry heard the sounds of death—heard Conrad's piercing scream, heard the thud, his contact with the rocky base. Terry's approach interrupted his memory. He took a brief look and then began practicing his leap to confirm that he could fly across the five-foot expanse.

Like Conrad yesterday. A shiver ran down Perry's back. *Is the devil here to claim another victim? Got to get out of here.*

Perry thrust his fear aside. He said, "Guys, let me show you something." While Terry continued his practice jumping, he led Victor, Graham, and Brayden to the narrowest part of the divide. Perry directed their attention across the ledge to reveal their goal. Pointing to the farthest point on the ledge across the divide, Perry said, "Conrad told me that's where he saw a sunny plain, a small sandy beach, and a beautiful lake. We'd have a place to swim. A good change from the long, dark, damp tunnels. Like coming to a holiday resort, he said."

Victor confirmed that their rope would bridge the gap. By hanging on to the rope, one could easily swing across the gap and climb the other side.

Graham and Brayden shook their heads. Perry looked skeptical too.

The boys returned to find Terry optimistic about his chances of making the jump. Victor practiced a few jumps to satisfy himself that he'd clear the divide.

"Well?" asked Terry.

"I should be able to make the jump, but we don't want to be too optimistic," said Victor.

Perry asked to pray for safety first, safety for all of them to make the crossing without a mishap. His prayer was short but welcomed by Brayden and Graham.

Then Terry made a mad dash for edge of the ledge. He leaped high into the air and sailed over the divide landing a comfortable distance on the opposite ledge. The boys cheered.

Like Conrad, thought Perry. *The real danger has yet to come.*

Victor led the boys to the far end of their ledge to the narrowest divide. He tossed his backpack, his sleeping bag, and some supplies across the divide. Terry collected them. Then Victor threw the rope. Terry trapped it under his foot, picked it up, and called out, "Ready when you are."

Victor faced his three skeptics. Perry, Graham, and Brayden had already backed away. Without hesitating, Victor instructed them on what he knew they knew. Taking up the slack in the rope, he said, "Just bring your legs up into a squat position. That will start you sailing across. As you near the far wall, bring your knees up to your chest and let your legs absorb the shock. The distance is short so there won't be much of an impact. After that, climb to the top where Terry will haul you in. Easy."

Victor saw a blank expression on two of the three faces. Ignoring their doubts, he looked to Terry and called out, "Ready?"

"Aren't you jumping across?" asked Terry.

"I thought I'd give these guys a demonstration."

Terry looked around frantically.

"Hold on," he called out.

He thought that when Perry, Graham, and then Brayden swung over, he'd have Victor with him to help pull the boys up. Now he needed a place to anchor the rope. How else could he hold Victor's two hundred-pound body? A large boulder behind him was too far away. A few steps back he saw a fracture in the ledge's surface. It was deep enough to jam his foot.

Possible to brace myself. I'll have to really lean back if I'm going to hold on to Victor.

Still worried, Terry drew up the slack and positioned himself for the challenge. He called, "Ready."

Victor did as he described. He stepped off the ledge and swung to the opposite wall. His legs absorbed the impact. Then, using his arms, he pulled himself up the rope and climbed on to the ledge and stood up.

"Whew! Didn't think it would work," said Terry.

Victor called out, "Okay. Who's next?"

I can't do that. Perry remembered the struggle he had in phys. ed. when he had to do chin ups. He barely made the minimum twenty chin-ups. *And that was a few years ago.*

Perry looked at Brayden and Graham. Neither seemed inclined to step up.

I don't want to be stuck here. I've got to do this.

Perry tossed over his belongings, and with a show of confidence, he picked up the rope. For a moment, he watched Victor carry his gear away. Then Perry looked down to the bottom of the divide. His legs refused to move.

Oh no. That was a mistake.

Terry noted Perry's reluctance. He called to Perry but received no answer. He tightened the rope's slack. Perry didn't move. Terry pulled harder. Perry resisted. "A tug-of-war?" he called out.

Perry's response was swift. "Not funny."

"Sorry." Terry eased pressure on the rope. "You decide when you're ready."

Victor stepped up and also picked up the rope. "This help?" he called out.

Perry looked at Brayden and Graham. He guessed, *If I don't make this jump, they won't either. That will mean the group will be divided or Terry and Victor will have to come back.* Remembering Conrad's failure in making the return jump, Perry committed to taking the challenge. With a nod to Terry, he followed Victor's example. The ease by which his legs absorbed the impact surprised him. Then Victor and Terry pulled him up.

Victor grabbed Perry's hand and hauled him on to the ledge. "Safe," he whispered, patting Perry on the back. Nodding to Graham and Brayden, he said, "Now show them they can do it too."

Looking at Victor, Perry said, "I still feel like I'm in the devil's backyard."

Victor smiled. "Show them."

"Easier than you think," Perry shouted.

"Who's next?" called Terry with the rope in his hand.

Neither Graham nor Brayden answered.

"Come on, guys. If Perry can do it, then each of you can do it."

No response. Terry looked at Victor for a suggestion. Seeing none, he pulled the rope to himself. His message to Graham and Brayden was clear—you're stuck there by yourself. After a few moments, Terry threw one end of the rope over the gap.

Graham quickly stepped on the rope before it slid over the edge. With his free hand, he tossed over his duffel bag and sleeping bag. He watched Victor take them out of his way and then grab the rope. Without any more delay, he followed Perry's example.

"Your turn," said Terry, tossing the rope to Brayden. Like Graham, Brayden stepped on the rope, tossed his belongings across the divide, and followed Graham's example. When he stepped on to the ledge, he was met with cheers.

"We did it, guys. Now, what's next?" asked Terry pointing to a tunnel opening.

"No," said Perry. "Let's check out the lake that Conrad talked about." He walked to the far end of the ledge. The boys followed his lead. The sight of the lake and the prospect of going for a swim painted a smile on their faces.

"But how do we get down there?" asked Brayden, looking at the steep graveled slope and a short fissure separating them from the slope.

"That's your concern? It's only about two feet." Terry pointed to the breach between them and the slope. The expression on Brayden's face confirmed his suspicion. "That's an easy jump, really only a skip."

"For you," said Brayden in a low tone.

"Brayden, you can do it. You'll see. After a couple of practice jumps, you'll see." Terry nodded to confirm his confidence in Brayden.

"It's the slope that worries me," said Perry. "It's not something we can walk down. It's too steep."

"I agree, but we can slide down on our butt." Terry looked at Perry for his reaction.

"That slope will force us to crash down, not slide." Perry shook his head.

"Maybe we could dig our heels into the gravel, slow the descent." Graham's suggestion came across as an out-loud thought.

"Good idea," said Victor.

Graham looked up surprised that the others heard him.

"You don't want to check out that tunnel first?" asked Brayden, pointing to the opening behind them.

"Haven't you had enough of tunnels yet?" The tone of Perry's response left no doubt about his feelings. Nods from the other boys confirmed Perry's objection.

Terry took charge by setting up a few rocks to represent the distance of the small fissure. Victor made the first practice jump with little trouble. Perry did the same. Graham's loping run resulted in him landing a one-foot distance.

"Graham, get serious." Terry's reaction came even before his friend stood up to see how well he'd done. "Run. Run like a bear is after you. You should land somewhere in the middle of that slope, not its edge."

Graham's next two attempts received Terry's full approval. Brayden took three practice jumps before he reluctantly admitted that he could do it.

Thinking that the other boys might still need more than Terry's enthusiasm, Victor volunteered to be the first to make the jump. "If I make it to the bottom safely, you'll toss my stuff over?"

"If?" asked Brayden.

"When," corrected Victor. "When I get safely to the bottom."

"Right," said Terry, wanting to rebuild their confidence.

Victor looked at the challenge before him. He was certain of the jump. The speed of going down the slope worried him. He didn't want to discourage Graham, Perry, or Brayden.

Victor took a longer run than he needed. He sailed comfortably over the divide and landed on his back, winded in the middle of the graveled slope. The second after he landed, his descent began. So did the sheet of gravel that he landed on. The huge sheet was a foot thick.

The farther Victor slid from his friends, the faster he went. He dug in his heels. No effect. He jammed his foot harder into the gravel. Worry gripped his face, a face the boys at the top couldn't see. A growing cloud of dust billowed behind him. When it finally settled, the boys saw Victor step away from the edge of the slope. He waved his arms.

Terry responded, saying to his friends, "Like a toboggan ride down a hill. This will be fun." He tossed Victor's sleeping bag and backpack as far as he could down the gravel slope. Immediately, they began rolling, then bouncing down the slope. Each time the bags hit on the surface, a few rocks joined the downward trek. The boys watched Victor's belongings race to the floor. After they crashed on the sandy floor, Victor picked them up and moved them away.

"I'm next," said Terry excited.

He received no objection.

"This is going to be fun." He tossed some of their supplies down the slope then asked Perry to throw his belongings down after he got to the bottom.

Like Victor, Terry's jump placed him in the middle of the graveled section, their perceived drop zone. Immediately, another thick sheet of gravel began its downward journey. Terry looked back and shouted, "This is like riding a gunnysack down the slide at the fair." Terry's ride picked up speed. "Y-a-h-o-o-o-o-o-o," shouted Terry.

Perry threw the rest of Terry's belongings down the grade. Tiny clouds of dust rose with the landing of the sleeping bag and carry-on bags. Then Perry threw his possessions.

"Second thoughts?" Brayden asked. He suspected Perry was throwing his gear down first because he was reluctant to make the jump, a feeling Brayden struggled with.

"Staying is not an option," said Perry. He backed up for a long run. Then he dashed toward the fissure, leaped high, and sailed into the air landing hard on the gravel. Immediately, he felt himself being carried forward, carried down the slope. He dug his heels deep into the gravel. No effect. Air brushed his face. He flew down faster than he wished, but the ride was smooth. He feared a jarring landing. As soon as he reached the bottom, he lost his balance and rolled several feet. The dust settled. Perry slowly stood up, shoulders banged up, back sore, and knees burning in pain. He waved to the friends at the top. When they waved back, he grinned.

No reason for them not to jump, he thought.

Then Terry and Perry dragged all their belongings part of the way toward the lake, adding them to Victor's pile. Terry hurried back and signaled the boys to throw their things down the slope. Four bags bounced wildly, small clouds of dust rising each time they hit the surface. When everything finally came to a stop, Terry waved for Graham and Brayden to come.

Graham walked back for his run. Brayden didn't.

"Something wrong?" asked Graham.

For a while, Brayden didn't answer. "I don't know. Something doesn't seem right."

"Something. What kind of something?"

Brayden shrugged.

"The jump?" Graham looked at the gravel and the five-foot hollow that had formed from where Victor and Terry had landed. He thought of it as a secure baseball glove.

"No," answered Brayden.

"The ride down?"

"There's no control. I can't help feeling I'll be like those bags, bouncing crazily all over the place." Brayden stepped away from the fissure as if he was afraid it was going to reach up and pull him in. "See that boulder?" He pointed to a large rock protruding two-thirds of the way down. The partially exposed boulder hadn't been visible when Victor and Terry made their jump.

"Yeah?"

"I can see being smashed into it. With the speed I'd be flying down, I'll be killed." Brayden looked past the rock to Terry waving frantically. He looked away.

Graham returned to Brayden's side. "Don't worry. The flow of the gravel sheet bypasses it. Perry had no problem with it."

"He was lucky."

"Then you'll be lucky too."

"Maybe my luck has run out."

"Let's jump together. We'll look out for each other."

Brayden's face brightened. "We'd run and jump at the same time?"

"Sure. We'll land close together." Graham nudged Brayden to their take off point. Using Terry's thinking, he said, "Let's race." Brayden looked up at his friend, smiled, and took off. Together, they sailed into the air and landed with a solid thud.

A massive, thick gravel sheet carried them forward, slowly at first. As the speed picked up, the ground shook beneath them. A roar grew from behind them.

Brayden desperately wanted to look back, but he was afraid of where he was being dragged. The wind whipped in his face. The avalanche roar grew louder.

More than halfway down, a huge rock bounced past them and grazed the protruding boulder. From the corner of his eye, Brayden saw a host of smaller rocks pelt the boulder. Brayden saw Terry turn and run, the boulder in hot pursuit, like a huge bowling bowl aimed at the last pin. The distance between the boulder and Terry decreased rapidly. Then Terry lay crushed, the boulder careening away like an escaping thief. The gravel sheet that Brayden and Graham rode charged down and hit the bottom of the slope. They tumbled. Before they could rise, hundreds of rocks that were sliding behind them pounded their bodies. Pain. Darkness enveloped them.

"No," shouted Perry. Trying to control his disbelief, he said under his breath, "The devil struck again."

The dust settled. Perry and Victor looked briefly at the boulder that had raced passed them. Then they stared at Terry's mangled corpse.

Unreal. This didn't happen.

Blood from Terry's crushed body testified to the opposite. Perry and Victor closed their eyes.

Moments later, they ran over to the spilled stones from the gravel avalanche and frantically searched for some sign of Brayden and Graham. For an hour, they crawled around the bed of rocks dumped at their feet. No sign of their friends, no indication that their friends were buried beneath the rocky rubble. Sitting on a spot where Brayden and Graham should have been, they cried. They recalled memories of their friends.

An hour passed. Perry mumbled, "We should say a prayer for them, for all of them."

"First, let's burry Terry. We'll pile a bunch of rocks over his body."

Perry nodded. At first, they carried two or three rocks at a time, not wanting to rush through their job, a means of showing respect for Terry's remains. Finally, after ignoring unmerciful back pains and complaining muscles, they rolled two large rocks to serve as a marker for Terry's resting place. Terry's duffel bag topped one of the rocks in place of a cross.

After Perry's longer than usual prayer, a prayer that dwelt heavily on the pain of their loss, Perry ended by saying, "I don't ever want to lead another memorial service again."

Victor hugged his friend. Without a word, they carried their possessions and Terry's sleeping bag to a tall rock near the lake. Leaning against the rock, they faced the boulder that killed their friend, watched the rock like it might yet come alive and come after them. The sun sank into the horizon taking its heat.

At first, they remained beside the large rock near the lake, their sleeping bag unzipped and draped over them. Aching muscles arrested any movement. The loss of their friends numbed their minds. The evening's temperature dropped. They curled up close to each other. No wood for a fire. Victor placed Terry's sleeping bag over them. Under its warmth, exhausted eyes closed.

CHAPTER 15

So Close

The emotionally exhausted boys greeted the morning sun. Victor and Perry stared at their new surroundings, not moving. Convinced any effort they made would be to their detriment, they just stared at the sky, at the flight of an occasional bird. They listened to the lake's waves lapping on the shore but said nothing.

The absence of Terry, Brayden, and Graham robbed them of yesterday's anticipation. Swimming. Playing in the lake. Drained of any goals, their rested bodies absorbed the warmth from their sleeping bags. Peace lay in doing nothing.

We're free from the tunnel's torment. A hollow victory, thought Perry.

Noon hour's heat radiating from the boulder and the ground forced the boys to seek shade. Once out of his sleeping bag, Perry mechanically prepared pancakes. He wasn't hungry. Neither was Victor.

IN THE END

They went for a swim, not to play, but as exercise. As a means of convincing themselves that swimming across the lake was not an option. After drying off, they propped themselves under the shady side of the boulder that they slept near.

Every now and then they shared a memory of Arny, or Sampson, or Len or ... They avoided discussing the only other topic that was important—where was Vanna? Verbalizing that goal meant setting themselves up as a target.

"Jean sure stuck to his guns," began Victor. "No one else went with him to work tunnel B. He went anyway." He paused. "Did I ever tell you about the time that Jean missed one of our canasta evenings?"

Perry shook his head.

"Six of us usually got together for cards Sunday evenings. One day, the church scheduled a special service. Arny suggested we play Monday night. We'd forgotten that Jean always visited his ill Uncle Elmer. Jean didn't join us that night."

"Guess that's why Sampson took on the task of always remembering our commitments," said Perry. "I know he really felt bad about Jean being left out. Jean had started feeling like he was part of our group."

"And Sampson did a good job," added Victor.

A little later, Perry talked about Arny. "Arny never complained about his swollen ankle. Not once. He must have been really down when he couldn't join us exploring the tunnels. He usually was the first to volunteer. He still tried to make himself useful. He poured though the mystery men's journal. You know, a lot of that stuff was boring."

"Arny never let challenges deter him," said Victor.

Victor's thoughts turned to Len and how well he accepted Victor's words of caution when Len teased Brayden about being afraid to swim. *And he had a good sense of humor.*

"Len was good at remembering people's names," said Perry. Len had served suppers at the Salvation Army. A couple of the down-and-out men told me that Len made them feel important. Not only did Len know them by name, but he remembered details about their lives and asked them about it. "He had a real heart for people."

Specific stories about each of their friends surfaced. They spoke of nothing else until the sun began to set.

Victor broke the pattern of the day's conversation. He suggested that next day they take their things and walk around the lake. No mention of Vanna. Just go out and see what was on the other side of the lake.

Early in the morning, Victor went for swim, saw many fish, and wished for a boat. "I could drop a line and just sit out there all day," he told Perry when they were eating. "Be a welcome change from pancakes."

Perry cleaned up. Victor packed up their belongings. Before beginning their walk, they stopped at Terry's burial site and wished him a good day. At the foot of the landslide, they said good-bye to Graham and Brayden. They left without looking back. Perry carried his sleeping bag and duffel bag, and Victor carried the rest of their supplies.

A relaxed walk. A sightseeing time. For most of the morning, only the lake on the left and a sandy waste on the right. Noon arrived. So did a grassland. The change began with scrawny tufts of grass here and there. Then long thin green ground cover crept closer to the lake. They redirected their walk to the soft sand to avoid being tangled in the long grass, sometimes getting their feet wet. Waves of heat rose from the afternoon's sun-soaked ground. To cool off, the boys took a swim. No playing around.

After a long walk, they came to a bend in the shoreline. They saw a cultivated field. Hopes of finding Vanna sprang up.

"Looks like wheat," said Victor. "Wish Graham was here. He'd know. He is a walking encyclopedia."

Perry noted Victor's use of the present tense in his last sentence. He chose not to correct Victor.

They plodded ahead. The joy of the cultivated field began to evaporate. No sign of equipment, a barn, a storage shed, or a house. No sign of human habitation.

"This isn't natural," said Victor, pointing to the rows of grain. "Someone planted this field."

"Considering the size of this field, I'd say with some machine," added Perry." All he could see was sky and grain.

"Sure would give anything for a set of wings," said Victor. He jumped into the air to see if he could see the end of the field. It didn't help. He shook his head.

They walked for what felt like forever, seeing nothing but lake to one side and grain opposite. Then in the distance, two rocky structures appeared, one tall and narrow. The other, farther away, a huge mound.

"That's our goal," said Victor, pointing to the rocky tower. "Maybe from there we can actually see an end to this field."

"And Vanna," added Perry. He looked back from where they had come.

After another hour's walk, Victor became concerned. The shoreline turned away from what he hoped would be a lookout tower. He estimated the walking time to the tower. *Too long to reach today.* He decided they would make camp, rest, and get an early start in the morning.

"Standing seeds of grain like grains of sand in the dessert. This seems to go on forever," said Victor, pointing to the far horizon. "Somewhere there must be a shed to house the machinery that did all this planting."

Thinking that this was his last chance for a swim, he dove into the lake. Here it was shallower than the last time he went for a swim. He saw several fish. After a half hour of swimming, it occurred to him there was a fishing line and hooks in their supplies. He had taken it from Sampson's father's tool kit.

It's worth a try.

Victor swam to shore. Inside of ten minutes, he was back in waist-deep water with lure dangling from a buoy a few feet away from him. Every now and then, he'd pull the line in and throw it out to a different spot.

He recalled wading into the Vermillion River with his uncle to catch fish. In silent competition his uncle, his father and he hoped to net the first catch. They'd look at each other and grin pretending that their choice of bait and the spot they chose would make them the winner. Bragging rights. It was fun.

May not catch anything tonight.

He had no bait. An hour passed by. No nibble. He thought he was wasting his time.

Fish are too smart or not hungry, maybe I should try later this evening.

Bored but not wanting to give up, he decided to try for another half hour.

Fish for supper sure would be nice.

He recalled the five in the morning wake-up time he endured. Cost to go out fishing at Cold Lake with his father and Uncle Bob. For more than half the morning drive, he slept in the back seat. Sometimes he'd wake up when his dad pulled up to the lake. Sometimes they'd wake him for breakfast. They'd have built a small fire, boiled water, and made coffee, a lot of coffee. Some of that coffee filled a thermos to drink when they were out in the boat. Breakfast. Coffee and toast with a thick layer of strawberry jam, an open strawberry sandwich.

"A sandwich," he had said. "For breakfast?"

"You think you're at a restaurant," his father countered. Victor never complained again.

Then his father and uncle paddled the motorboat on the lake. "Don't want to alert the fish," his father said. His father and uncle quietly dipped the oars into the water and nudged their boat away from shore, sometimes drifting, sometimes paddling. Once they reached "the spot" —Victor never knew how they knew where that spot was—the lines were baited and cast. No talking time.

"Don't wanna scare away the fish," his uncle instructed.

Then it was daydream time, sip some coffee, daydream some more. "That's when they'll bite," said Uncle Bob quietly. "When you least expect it."

And sure enough. When your mind was a million miles away, the line would jerk. The fun began.

One morning while fishing at Cold Lake, Victor got the first bite. *At the time I was thinking of bidding in a poker game with Larry, Len, Arny, and Sampson at Len's home. My fishing pole jumped. I scrambled to hang on to it. Then I worked my catch close to the boat. Uncle Bob netted the walleye. I caught two more fish that day. Uncle Bob caught five. It was a good day, a day Uncle Bob liked to recall months later.*

Slipping out of his reverie, Victor looked at his bobbing buoy. *No luck.* He tossed the line out in another direction thinking, *Last time*, for the third time. A few seconds after, the lure sank below the water's surface; the buoy dived after it.

"Got one," Victor shouted, loud enough for Perry to hear.

Hand over hand, Victor pulled supper in. He carried it to shore. Perry met him with the skillet in hand. One skillet whack killed the fish. Victor filleted it. Perry cooked it. He admitted that Victor won their bet. Victor did catch a fish.

The next morning, Victor woke up to a bright blue sky, caressing cool air, and the lake's lapping waves inviting him for an early swim. *Just like a resort.* The warm sun's rays promised an early oven atmosphere making the swim more compelling.

They discussed the day's plan—hike for several hours. "But before breakfast, we can afford a half hour in the lake," said Victor.

Perry resisted the temptation. He wanted to complete their trek before the afternoon heat beat down on him.

Victor dove into the lake but promptly returned to shore when Perry called. As soon as they finished their meal, Victor packed up and led the way into the grain field. The plants were almost knee-high. His intent to angle his way to the rocky lookout tower changed after the first half hour. Resistance in stepping across the rows made Victor choose to walk with the rows. He knew the increased distance would add time to their destination, but it would be less draining on Perry.

Silent progress. When the sun was almost directly over them, they were almost halfway to their goal. The sun's rays beat down unmercifully.

From the soft sandy soil rose waves of heat mixed with dust. Perry coughed then walked thirty paces behind Victor. Perspiration streaked the dust on his face. Victor shortened the length of his steps so as not to leave Perry too far behind. He stopped for their second break, a break for Perry. When they restarted their trek, Victor carried Perry's duffel bag containing the food and the stove. Perry didn't object. Victor hoped Perry could handle his sleeping bag and the coiled rope.

By the midafternoon stop, they were perpendicular to their goal. The tower displayed two ledges. Victor hoped the lower ledge would allow him to see the end of the field and maybe some sign of human habitation. He ignored the second distant rocky rise, the one that looked like a very high plateau.

For now, they still had hours of feet sinking into soft soil before they reached the tower. Crossing the rows would slow them down. Looking back at the tramped path they made, Victor noted that they had actually angled away from his goal. Not much, but enough to add at least another half hour to their walk. Shrugging, he began breaking a trail at right angles to the rows.

Perry faithfully trudged breathing heavily, but not saying a word about his splitting headache. Intense heat did that to him. At home, he'd always wore a cap. When he went to the boy's man cave, the forecast was rain. Who needed a cap?

To keep up, Perry endeavored to step in each of Victor's footprints. That forced him to focus on the ground, a good thing. Seeing how far away he was from the tower had depressed him, made him want to give up. Counting when he successively stepped into Victor's foot imprint distracted him. He'd turned it into a game. He was so absorbed in his challenge that he didn't notice how close he was to their goal until the ground changed from tilled soil to gravel. Then came Victor's, "Almost there."

Their walk took longer than Perry anticipated. Looking beyond Victor's shoulder, Perry marveled at the height of the spire of sedimentary rock. He estimated it rose at least sixty feet. The top of the tower leaned slightly away from them beyond its base. For a moment, he thought of the climbing walls that Arny, Calvin, and Victor used to scramble up at the gym. Then he caught sight of the shade on one side of the tower.

Relief.

Perry hurried passed Victor. He unrolled his sleeping bag, curled up one end for a pillow, swallowed some warm water, and stretched out on the ground, his head pounding. Safe from the sun's rays, he stared up at the blue sky. No birds. No clouds, but after a few minutes, he thought he felt a slight drop in temperature. Victor followed Perry's example. A smile crossed Perry's face.

Good. I'm not the only one who needs a rest. No way I'm moving from here.

He heard Victor's exhausted admission. Silence followed. Then more words, something about the other rocky area a few miles away.

Did Victor mumble something about scaling up to the first ledge?

Perry's eyes remained closed. He heard nothing else. He missed hearing Victor move his sleeping bag into the sun or him saying he wanted to study the rock face, map out a possible route to the lower ledge.

Once Victor stretched out on his sleeping bag and rested his head on a part of Terry 's sleeping bag, he began examining the rock face.

Good angle. My weight will press into the rock's face. Be easier to climb.

The lower ledge drew his attention. It stretched two-thirds of the way across the front of the rock. To get there, he'd have to climb almost halfway up the rocky structure.

Hopefully from there I'll be able to see to the end of the grain field, maybe even see some buildings.

Dozens of holes varying in sizes were scattered beneath the ledge. Some cavities appeared large enough to support a foothold. Others a hand grip. No protruding rocks for foot support like the climbing wall in the gym.

Picking a path to the first ledge still should be no trouble.

Victor fought the urge to immediately tackle the challenge. Letting his muscles recover from their long trek made sense. The view he looked forward to would still be there in an hour.

He stood up and approached the tower for a closer look. A route up the wall began to develop.

IN THE END

How easy would it be to make the climb? I could try a foot or two.

The first couple hand and foot grips came easy. So did the third and fourth. His muscles offered no complaint. Seeing more opportunities to extend his climb, Victor pushed his body up another three feet, then another three feet. This continued until he firmly planted himself on the ten-inch-wide ledge. He examined the layers of sedimentary rock that he stood on. No cracks. No holes. He edged his way along the ledge until he rounded a small bend.

The entire grain field came into view. It stretched to the horizon. Victor strained his eyes. No building. No machinery. Only a grain carpet.

Got to go higher.

Victor searched for new grips, grips that would take him up another twenty feet to the next ledge.

It has to offer a better view.

Holes large enough to accept his foot appeared less frequently and farther apart. At times, he settled for only a toehold. Progress slowed. One foot, then a second, then a third. As his left foot reached up for the next support only a few inches away, the hole supporting his right foot gave way. Victor's full weight transferred to his hands. His hands slipped. He dropped. Face and hands scraped the rock. Feet blindly searched for support. Then a foot slammed on to the lower ledge, a protruding portion. Within a few seconds, it gave way.

His descent restarted. Victor's left hand shot out and caught a hold of a hole. His grip didn't last. Victor's waist slid past the ledge. His left hand reached out and grabbed the ledge. His right hand did the same. There he hung, feet dangling, searching for some kind of support. His feet found none. Victor looked up.

If only I could pull myself up to that ledge…

Was there another hole above the ledge that he could use to lift himself? He saw one. It was one a few inches higher.

Reachable, he thought.

Strained muscles dragged his body a few inches up the rock's sloping face.

Next. Right hand reaches up and grabs a new hold. If this works, I might eventually climb onto that ledge.

Victor's right hand eased its hold on the ledge to see if his other arm could hold him in place.

Friction of my body against the rock should keep me in place.

His full weight transferred to the left arm for only a couple of seconds. He couldn't do it. Both arms were needed to hold him up.

Must have a foothold.

He slid his right toe to the right and left, then up a little, then right and left, and up a little again. His search offered no grip. Afraid that the left foot would give the same result, Victor admitted he was in trouble. Looking at a jagged piece of rock sticking out from the broken ledge, he wished for such a hold above the ledge.

With a rope tied to it I could inch my way up to the ledge. A rope. We have one. Perry has rope.

He imagined Perry standing on the ledge above him pulling him up with a rope.

"Perry," he shouted. Hearing nothing, he repeated his cry two more times.

"Holy cow," exclaimed Perry from the base of the tower.

He came. Victor looked down but couldn't see his friend. "I need your help."

"Anything."

Perry's quick response assured Victor that he had a hope.

"Get our rope and bring it up to the ledge."

Silence greeted Victor's request.

Had Perry immediately run off for the rope? Was he in shock? When he was working out at the gym, he always avoided the climbing wall.

"Perry, you there?"

Victor heard no response. He waited, afraid of the answer. Victor listened for some sound from Perry. His arm muscles ached, the joints in his shoulder screamed for relief.

This situation can't last. He called again, "Perry."

"Yeah."

"How you doing?"

"I'm halfway up. Just hang on."

Victor told himself that Perry would make it. He had the knowledge. Perry had heard Arny and Calvin talk often enough about how to pick your way up a wall. Victor stared at the slab of rock in front of his nose. The hope that help was close by renewed his resolve, made the pain tolerable.

It won't be much longer.

A voice from above him broke his concentration. "I'm here."

Victor looked up. Perry was standing a couple of feet away from the broken ledge, the coiled rope hung from his shoulder.

"I can't pull you up," said Perry, his face wry.

"That's okay. I only need you to be an anchor."

Only. What an understatement.

Perry standing on the ledge would make it possible for him to climb up on to the ledge. Victor knew he'd still have to hoist himself high enough to get his knees on the ledge, but if he could do that, he should be able to climb on to the ledge.

Pull myself up.

A major challenge for his sore arms. A challenge he must accomplish. Failure meant he'd plunge to his death.

No choice.

"Here's what I want you to do. Throw one end of the rope to me. Actually, throw the rope on my right hand. Then brace yourself. While holding on to the ledge with one hand I'll quickly grab the rope with the other hand. That way my weight won't be a shock for you. When I completely let go of the ledge, you'll have to counter-balance my weight."

"Lucky I weigh more than you do," said Perry with a forced chuckle. As he listened to his friend, he slid the rope off his shoulder.

"I'm counting on that. Don't let me win this contest."

Perry's first three tosses fell short of Victor's hands. The next two rolled off his hand. The sixth time he lowered the rope until it rested on Victor's hand. Victor's "good" initiated Perry's crouch. Victor's right hand grabbed the rope. His fingers scraped the ledge. He muffled an "ow."

"Tell me before you plan to grab the rope with your other hand so that I can really lean back." Perry prayed. Then he remembered how sharply Terry leaned when Victor swung over the narrow gap between him and Terry. Terry's success boosted his confidence.

"On three," said Victor. After Perry's answer, he shouted, "One," He paused. "Two." He paused. "Three."

Victor's left hand seized the rope. Perry's hold held. Without letting go of the rope, Victor slid his right hand up a few inches. The sound of his shirt rubbing on the rock assured him of progress. After sliding his left hand up to the right hand, he pulled himself up, then repeated the process. Inches became a foot and a foot became a second foot. He could see all of Perry's feet. Then Victor's runner found a hole in the wall, a hole large enough for most of his foot to slip into. Immediately, his leg eased the pressure on his arms.

What a relief. Thank God.

Life-giving energy flowed into Victor's arms. While standing on one leg, his other foot rubbed up and down on the rock face.

Where there's one hole, there's got to be another.

Early attempts failed. Then he repeated his efforts using a grid search, a search that began close to his leg. Near his knee, he found a second hole. His foot easily slid into it. Up he went. His knee was getting close to the ledge.

Only another two feet. Then I can put my knee onto the ledge.

Another grid search. First the right foot. Then the left foot. No success.

Oh no. Back to hoisting myself.

Now it was easier. His arms had a needed break. Success was so close.

I can do this.

Pain in his arms screamed for relief.

Only for a few more minutes.

A knee found the ledge.

Made it.

With Perry's help, he pulled himself to a standing position.

"We did it." A smile lit up Victor's face. He looked at the dried blood on his knuckles.

"Thank God," said Perry, standing upright. He gave the rest of the rope for Victor to gather up. Together, they shuffled their way around the bend in the ledge. When they got to the spot where Perry had climbed on to the ledge, Perry said, "I don't know how to get down."

"What do you mean? The same way you came up."

"Coming up was easy. I could see where to put my hands, my feet. Going down I can't see anything.

On the wall at the gym, you can see where to put your feet."

To Perry, the drop meant death or worse—a broken arm and leg. Being a cripple in this wilderness would be a slow torture.

"All you have to do is feel around with the tip of your foot. There are many holes. Your eyes will show you where to stick your hands."

"Victor, I can't see me doing it. If I have to hang on for a long time, my arms will give out. You've got to help me."

Perry's pleading meant more instructions weren't likely to convince him to start climbing down.

"I'll tell you what. I'll be your eyes. I'll start going down first. You'll follow. I'll tell you exactly where to place your feet."

Victor's plan met with Perry's approval. Together, they worked their way down to solid ground. Victor let his arms hang down.

Feels so good.

"Thanks," said Victor. "I know climbing up there took a lot of courage for you. I really appreciate it."

"Well," stated Perry, "I'd like to say it was nothing, but it was better than the alternative."

"The alternative?"

"Yeah. Remember. I told you I didn't want to do another memorial service."

Perry's smile told Victor he was kidding.

CHAPTER 16

At Last

Heat radiated off the rocks. Shade was less than one hundred steps away. Without a word being said, Perry and Victor moved to the other side of the tower.

Once they were safe from the sun's burning rays, Perry pointed to the ground and told Victor to sit down. Without waiting for a response, Perry pulled off his sweat soaked T-shirt and found a dry part that had hung below his waist. He reached into his duffel bag, pulled out a water bottle, and began soaking the dry part.

Still standing, Victor said, "What are you doing?"

"If you had a mirror, you'd know. Your face is a mess. Blood all over it." He put a hand on his friend's shoulder. "Now sit down while I clean you up."

"Don't make your shirt dirty. Use mine."

Stepping back from Victor, Perry pointed to Victor's dirty shirt. It was ripped in many places. "Really."

Victor carefully eased himself to the ground. Perry gently placed his wet shirt on Victor's forehead and waited for the dried blood to be absorbed. He told Victor about something that looked like a stream running away from the distant high plateau.

"If I'm right, we can rinse our clothes and refill our water bottles before making our way to that summit."

"We're going to that plateau," Victor said, surprised at the certainty of Perry's statement.

"Well, you don't think you're going back up this tower. When I was up there, I saw very few places where you could find a grip to go higher."

"That doesn't mean it would be impossible." He groaned after Perry wiped away some blood.

"Sorry." Perry placed the cloth more gently on Victor's cheek. "I know you're anxious to get a better view of the area, but doing it from here is not an option. I don't want to go up there and rescue you again. That climb scared me."

"I'm sure it did. That was your first climb, and to a height almost doubled what we had in the gym. That took a lot of courage. Thanks again. You saved my life."

Mine too. Perry thought that if Victor had died, so would he. *I wouldn't try climbing any mountains. Instead, I'd wander around in this sea of grain. Probably die of thirst or hunger. It would be an agonizing death.*

Perry wiped the last of the blood from Victor's face. He carefully placed the wet cloth on Victor's bloody knuckles. When Perry finished, Victor stretched out on his sleeping bag. Rest felt so good.

They spent their time talking about their friends, what they liked best about each of them, ridiculous things they did. Finally, Perry decided to redirect their focus.

"You know the day we spent by the lake near the rockslide? I really enjoyed it."

Victor nodded. "Being out in the sun was a whole lot better than poking around in those dark tunnels."

"It was warm, we had a place to swim, and we may have had fresh food."

"Fish." Victor smiled. "Good menu change. I knew you would do a great job frying them."

"I would have been content to stay there." Perry checked Victor's facial expression.

Victor's smile disappeared. He looked at Perry to determine how serious he was. "For a while maybe." He let his comment comfort Perry. "But you know the fuel for our cooking stove is low. I'm guessing only a few days. Then we'd have to be eating raw fish. I'm not a fan of that."

"I get it. That's why we've got to keep pushing on to find Vanna." He turned away from Victor.

"Right. I'm hoping that when I get to the top of this next peak, I'll see something to give us a clear direction to other people."

Perry said nothing. He didn't want Victor to know that he he'd given up on finding Vanna. To hide his disappointment, he told Victor he was tired. Without waiting for a response, he curled up in his sleeping bag.

The next morning after breakfast, the boys walked out to the stream. Although the air was cool, Perry didn't wear his blood-stained T-shirt. It had to be rinsed. In the afternoon, he'd wear it to avoid a sun burn.

Perry knew his route wasn't the shortest distance to the plateau. He was adding at least an hour or two to their trek. Nothing to look forward to. Victor didn't object. Earlier, he surprised Victor when he had recommended that they follow the stream's meandering path to the base of the summit. In answer to Victor's "Why?" he explained he liked the sound and sight of the water. It suggested life, hope.

"I guess. We'll have access to fresh water for a longer time too," added Victor.

By late afternoon, they arrived at the foot of the plateau, the base being a massive hill of strewn boulders of various sizes. Too late to begin any climbing. They wouldn't reach the summit before nightfall. It was better to stay here and rest, better to sit back and watch the water pour out of a cavity twenty feet above the ground. The splashing sound gave Perry an idea. "Let's wade in the pool at the bottom of the rocky base." He wanted to avoid the long climb up the plateau. Perry knew he couldn't delay scaling the summit much longer, but a night's rest meant he might be able to handle the climb.

Am I pushing Victor's will to be flexible? Tomorrow he may insist upon reaching the top of the summit. That could mean full day of climbing in the heat. Once Victor committed himself to a course of action, he doesn't abandon it easily. He may not want to stop for rest breaks. Better enjoy this break. There might not be another chance.

As Perry suspected Victor was up early the next morning. "Better to hike in the cool air," he said. Victor confidently stepped up, over, and around rocks like he was a mountain goat out for a morning stroll.

"Coming?" he called back from a thirty-foot energetic lead. He didn't wait for a response. After working his way up another fifty feet, he looked back at Perry carefully plodding along.

From time to time, Perry's loosely strapped sleeping bag swung to his side, causing him to side-step. Victor shrugged. He'd offered to carry the cooking utensils and food—they only had another day or two of supply—but Perry said he wasn't helpless. By noon, Perry's pace slowed. He was ready to accept a break when Victor called out.

"Perry, you've got to see this. Hurry up."

Victor was one hundred feet ahead, but the incline was slight. Two hours earlier, Perry would have covered that distance in no time. Now, Victor sat on large boulder to wait for his struggling friend. As Perry neared him, Victor pointed down to his side and said, "Look at this." He gave no hint of the surprise awaiting Perry.

Perry approached his grinning friend. A huge open space appeared. Then he saw a heart-stopping precipice, one that overlooked a very long lake. Its dark blue color suggested a considerable depth.

"No doubt the source of water for that waterfall we saw below," said Victor.

"It's beautiful," said Perry, straightening his sore back.

They couldn't climb down to the lake because of the steep drop. The boys sat and admired the view. The last thing Perry wanted to hear was Victor's, "Time to go." It came too soon.

Victor didn't wait for Perry's input. He started picking his way up a long gradual incline away from the view of the lake. Perry figured out what Victor's goal was. Then he chose a different path, a path with a gentler slope. This route allowed him to frequently gaze down at the lake below but increased the distance between him and his friend. Perry's choice meant a very steep climb at the end. He'd handle it.

For the longest time, their meeting place was the furthest thing from Perry's mind. Every now and then, instead of gazing down at the lake, he would look up to see Victor's progress.

Not a problem. Victor still has a way to go.

The hot sun drained Perry. He sweat heavily. For a break, he stopped and bent back to see his friend. Victor was sitting on a boulder near the top, his three canteens and sleeping bag stacked on the ground beside him. Victor waved.

Perry's right arm reached up in response. His left shoulder dropped, and the sleeping bag slipped off his shoulder. Perry sidestepped. His foot twisted and forced him to lean left. He yelled but recovered in time to plant his foot on another rock, a little lower, a bit to his left. The rock rolled. Perry's other knee buckled. The sleeping bag plunged down the embankment. Desperately trying to prevent tumbling down Perry fell forward. As he slid, he grabbed two rocks jutting out of the ground. The rocks pulled free. Perry disappeared over the edge.

Victor scrambled down to where he last saw Perry. All he could see were ripples in the water. No sign of Perry. Only a sleeping bag, its strap caught on a rock near the bottom.

Victor sank to his knees. *This didn't happen. This couldn't happen.*

"No. No. No." His eyes closed, extinguishing the evidence of the fall. When he opened them again, the sleeping bag remained, testifying to the tragedy.

Drained of goals, of hopes, of ambition, of energy, Victor sat crumpled. A heap of nothing. He prayed for Perry, prayed he'd be with the rest of his friends, prayed he be safe in Vanna or heaven.

Slowly, reality sank in. *You're alone. By yourself. You've no one to count on but yourself. Be careful. Be very careful. You will have no more chances. One mistake and you will be gone like Perry, like Terry, like*

Graham, like Brayden, like ... He couldn't continue naming his missing friends.

Perry's words, "I would have been content to stay there," returned to Victor. *He would have been happy by that lake. He would have been alive. I could have been happy. We were out of those tunnels.*

Tears flooded Victor's vision. He blamed himself for pushing to find Vanna, for seeking a bird's-eye view of their area. He saw Perry's reluctance to start the climb in the morning, his objection to Victor's search.

He was too nice a guy to say anything. I should have taken the hint.

Wiping his eyes, Victor looked at the distant peak still beckoning him. He muted an urge to say, *It's your fault.* The possibility of sighting Vanna from that vantage point tugged at him.

Victor stood up and looked down at the snagged sleeping bag. As if talking to his friend he said, "I'll find Vanna. Your death won't be for nothing." Progress began with him picking his way up to the place where he had waved to Perry.

As he bent down to retrieve his sleeping bag, his eyes fell upon the boulder that he had sat on to watch Perry. He felt the boulder speak to him: "Just like that. You going to leave without spending time mourning where you lost your friend? Is finding Vanna that important to you?"

That last question burned. *Vanna is nothing without Perry, without Perry or any of my other friends.*

How useless is my effort to find Vanna? Victor sat on the boulder.

He thought of Perry from the moment Perry knew they were trapped in the underground tunnels. *Already then, he felt some malevolent force was out to get him. While we were in the tunnels, that feeling never left him. Even before we crossed that divide to the gravel slope, he suspected another death was imminent. He probably thought he was next. He only relaxed after a day at the lake. Probably felt safe, out of reach of the devil he'd say.*

Victor shook his head. *Perry wasn't afraid. True. He refused to go down some tunnels. Must have figured no good would come from it. Why risk your life for nothing? But when it came to rescue me on the face of that tower, he was there. He was brave. No doubt about it. He was brave.*

Victor had no idea how long he sat on the boulder, but he finally realized he was staring at the spot where he last saw Perry. He looked around. His shadow had moved. He tied the canteens to his belt and grabbed the sleeping bag. Steps toward the peak lacked the morning spring. Doubt clung to his feet as if they were being sucked back by deep wet mud.

Perry's dead. Was that my fault? Me pushing to find Vanna. What was so important about Vanna anyway? An ideal community. Big deal. How ideal could it be without all my friends? Maybe Vanna was a pot of gold at the end of the rainbow. Maybe a fiction. A fiction that cost Perry his life.

IN THE END

Almost out of breath, Victor stopped and looked back. His progress, only three hundred feet. No reason to be breathing so hard. His heart wasn't in the climb, but the need remained. Losing Perry hadn't left him.

I need to refocus. Think of something neutral, maybe something positive.

Placing his foot on a rock ten inches higher he thought of the last pool game he played in the man cave. Successful unexpected shots, missed shots, a need to knock Arny off his eight-game winning streak gave way to red pool balls rolling on the garage floor, the garage's sloping floor, Sampson crawling underneath to see outside the garage.

Had we fallen to the bottom of the hole, we might have all died from the impact. Or maybe we would have drowned. That might have been better than poking around in the dark tunnels wandering around refusing to accept reality. At least we'd have been in heaven. Sounding like Perry.

Victor began his climb. An hour later, labored breathing forced him to stop. Fighting the mountain's steeper incline and negative thoughts sapped his energy, his will to keep going.

How far have I gone? Count the steps. The higher the number, the farther I will have gone. A positive motivation.

Victor's new focus lifted his spirits. The fact that he had to start over four times didn't matter. That new challenge was, how far could he count before his concentration evaporated? The first time his attention flipped back to Perry he'd only taken 512 steps. A sense of accomplishment lifted his spirits when his counting reached 2,054. Marshalling his will power to be more attentive, he reached 2,804 steps before he realized his thoughts had returned to the tunnels. When Victor reached the summit, his count was at 3,490. His feeling of success diminished. He realized that the plateau he intended to reach was still a considerable distance away and higher up. A valley lay before him.

Exhausted, he emptied a canteen and found a flat surface to lie down on. The sleeping bag captured his body heat, and he fell into a deep sleep. In the morning, Victor woke up, not to the sun shining on his face but to the rumbling of an empty stomach. He had nothing to eat last night. Drinking half a canteen of water stilled the rumble.

He planned the day's challenge. A foothill-walk down to the valley floor. Easily doable. Shrubbery on the valley floor. Leaves would absorb some of the heat. The two- or three-mile walk should be relaxing. The lower slope on the opposite side appeared to be gentle, something to be walked up, not climbed. It was bare of foliage and exposed to the west sun. Victor was sure he'd be standing on the plateau by the end of the day. Maybe even looking down on Vanna or at least some indication of human habitation.

Victor began his trek confidently until he began working his way up the opposite slope. The burning sun baked the ground. Waves of heat enveloped him. When Victor was halfway up the slope, his perspiration-soaked shirt clung to his body. He emptied the second canteen of water. Wisdom said seek shade, but there was no shade. All he could do was move slowly and choose the least taxing path. Rest frequently and take only one swallow of water. His advances shrank from fifty feet to twenty feet to ten feet.

A large boulder appeared. A possibility of a hiding place from the sun's rays. After a ten-minute rest, Victor edged his way to the boulder. The shadow cast by the boulder stretched a foot beyond its base, enough area to shelter only his head. *Minimal relief.* Victor was cooking.

Looking ahead, he saw something unusual. He blinked twice hoping to clear his vision. It made no difference. A woolly line of gray traced itself up before reddish-brown rock. Its wavy shape dismissed the possibility that he was looking at a shadow from something. To see from where that oddity originated, he had to move ahead another twenty feet. Then he could see over the rise. He took a swallow of water. Leg muscles, back muscles ached. Half-crouching, he advanced. The gray form rose from a distant ground, one below his present location.

He knelt down in disbelief. *A mirage? Smoke?* If it was smoke, there would be somebody there, somebody with water, with food. He stared at the abnormality. It disappeared. He fixed its location, then examined the area that separated him— a shallow valley, much wider than the last one, little shrubbery, more exposure to the sun. If he crossed during the day, his half canteen of water wouldn't be enough to keep him hydrated. Especially during another hot day.

Victor looked at the sinking sun. The temperature had dropped slightly. With an hour's rest, he'd have enough energy to work his way down to the valley floor. After another rest and with light from the moon he could cross to the other side and begin the climb, maybe reach the rise where he saw what he thought was smoke. If only he could reach the summit before the sun rose and stole the rest of his strength. Maybe there would be a shadow where he could hide for at least a part of the day.

CHAPTER 17

Who Is Yazpar?

*I*t moved! I'm sure it did.

It. About a half mile away, a blue-green or maybe a gray-blue speck to the left of a boulder. The boulder sitting on the edge of a rocky ledge waiting for a gentle earthquake to nudge it crashing down over the cliff.

The first time Yazpar saw that oddity near the boulder, he was preparing supper. Thinking his eyes were playing tricks on him—they weren't what they used to be thirty years ago—he dismissed it. With his rough hand, he brushed the gray hair away from his eyes.

Imagination. Out in the sun too long.

As he ate his yam pancake topped with a thin layer of melted goat cheese and sipped his homemade blueberry wine, he checked on the speck again. No clearer, but it appeared on the right side of the boulder. He was certain it had moved. Without taking his eyes off the intruder he bit into his pancake and chose not to sip his wine lest he missed seeing the object change place. It didn't. Finally, he glanced down to pick up the other pancake and take a sip of wine. He checked on the ferric rocky ledge's guest. Still there. Same place.

Can't be a seed that has taken root in some loose shale. If a bush had sprouted, surely, I'd have seen it before. Too far to tell.

He finished his meal all the while watching for any sign of movement.

Wait. The speck was on the left side of the boulder before supper. It did move. Couldn't be a bush. Unless I was wrong, and it was on the right side.

Yazpar wished he had his binoculars. They were buried somewhere in one of the many packed boxes at the back of his storage area.

At one time, he used them to watch the Catolone boys haul two cases of wine to his shelter. *How skillfully they picked their way up the trail. Like mountain goats,* he thought smiling. That was two years ago. No longer teenagers but full-time workers in their father's winery. Their labor in the fields meant they were always in excellent physical shape. Lately, the boys climbed their way up. No racing. No bouncing from one sure-footed hold to another. *No more fun for anyone.*

He poured a little water on the smoldering ashes, stirred them, and poured more water. When he was certain his fire was out, he went in search of the wooden hawk he'd been carving. He scraped and cut fine feather lines on his bird until it was time to go to sleep. The sun was low but high enough to confirm that something was on the mountain. That speck had moved again, had reached the summit.

"Tomorrow," murmured Yazpar. "Tomorrow, we'll see."

***

Eyes opened.

Long salt-and-pepper beard, mustache covered lips. Too close.

Victor attempted to turn his head, but the neck muscles objected.

Full head of hair, gray and white. Bright blue sky backdrop. Morning?

Mouth smiled. Canteen.

Water!

Something lifted his head. A few drops of water splashed into his open mouth, then more. His voice croaked, "You real?" Victor feebly raised his hand and touched the sleeve of the man holding the canteen.

"As real as you are." Yazpar gently set his visitor's head to the ground. "My name is Yazpar."

Without thinking, Victor said his name. *Safe. At last.*

Eyes closed.

***

As soon as Yazpar was certain his exhausted visitor was asleep, he cleared off his spare cot. The cot was the recipient of some laundry, hand towels, a long gray woolen sweater he hadn't worn in four days and a painting kit. He dragged the metal cot to a shady spot where a gentle breeze blew. Picking up Victor, he placed him on the cot, then went inside to wash up. He took scissors and cut his beard a bit and trimmed his mustache. He had no company for the last few weeks. Why worry about grooming?

Yazpar looked in the mirror. Looked more acceptable. Victor was still sleeping so Yazpar ate his lunch alone.

He turned his attention to a new painting he started in the morning; a painting inspired by Victor's appearance. *A miracle,* he thought.

The boy had crossed a forbidding expanse, long valleys, demanding slopes. He shouldn't have survived, and yet he lived to tell about it.

Like a man who crossed the Sahara Desert on foot.

The presumed bush he thought he saw two days ago formed the foundation of his painting. His miracle impression. As he ate, plans took shape. He'd portray the different layers of sedimentary rock, create an impression of overwhelming barrenness.

Texture. Texture was important. The boulder, out of place, a puzzle. Make it smooth as if polished by rushing water from a river. And carried there perhaps before the earth quaked, perhaps carried there by Noah's flood.

The imagined bush fascinated him. It was the heart of his desire for this painting. The bush represented the boy. True, it would have to be small, insignificant, growing near the top of the folded rusty sedimentary sheets, but that spoke of the miracle of life. A seed finds sufficient nutrients in loose shale, particles of sand. Water from heaven and then a sprout pokes its head into the sun light. It shouldn't have happened, not there in that barren surface.

What a wonder!

Now, what would that bush look like? How high? How bushy? How thick the branches?

That will come.

He eyed the still-sleeping boy.

On a thick cream-stained cardboard, he began sketching the rocky base. It took more than two hours, not because he didn't know what to do, but he savored the complexity of the rock formation, its crevices, its shaded and morning-sun surfaces.

Once, Victor stirred. He accepted a few swallows of water from Yazpar, then closed his eyes, breathing normally.

Supper, when I'm done, thought Yazpar. *Easily done when I'm living by myself.*

The granular face of the mountainside first, then supper.

After studying his work and memorizing the details, he mixed an assortment of substances together producing a thick gummy paste. A two-inch putty knife spread the translucent glue-like material across the face of his sketched mountainside. The sticky layer began to dry. He mixed up a pot of crushed shale with a fluid gummy cream and added in a reddish grainy powder to thicken it. When the stirred paste thickened, he turned his attention to the tacky surface of his mountain. With a metal spoon, he tapped the gummy mountain surface until the glue resisted the spoon's withdrawal.

Victor stirred, then slowly sat up.

Oh no. Without turning around, he said, "There's a water jug by your head. Wine too, if you prefer. Got to finish here before everything dries."

His glance at the cot showed that Victor heard him. Victor had reached for the jug of water.

A second wide-bladed putty knife spread the reddish paste over half the mountain side. Then a square-headed stick chiseled lines across the paste, scraped crevices, and dug small holes here and there. Yazpar repeated the action for the top portion of his mountain face.

Two hours passed. During the latter hour, Victor walked over and, without saying a word, watched Yazpar complete the first part of his rocky scene. Yazpar set his tools down.

"You have an amazing talent. Your work looks so realistic."

"Thank you." Yazpar continued without looking up.

"May I ask you something?"

"Certainly."

"If you're representing the scene up there—" Victor pointed to the spot from where he first saw Yazpar's fire. "Why did you put a tree in there?" He pointed to the sketched bush on the mountain top of Yazpar's work. "Nothing's growing there."

"At the time, I had no idea what was up there. I certainly didn't expect a person. The only possibility was a bush. That didn't seem possible. I hadn't seen it there before, but as I said, it was all I could think of." He glanced up at Victor. Seeing no critical expression, he continued. "Something growing up there would be a miracle. But then you being up there was a miracle."

"I suppose painting a bush instead of a person is more realistic." Victor's muse was more for himself than Yazpar.

"So, why were you up there?" He turned and looked up at Victor.

"At that point, looking for you."

"But you didn't know I was here. What brought you there?"

"Vanna." The name slipped slowly, softly from Victor's lips as if he were afraid to admit he was searching for a place that he did not even know if it existed.

"Vanna. Really! I know it." Yazpar turned to his painting.

"You do." Victor's face lit up.

"Sure. It's a small city in the valley below, about a day's walk from here."

"That's what we've been searching for."

"We?" Yazpar turned around. "There's more of you?" His voice filled with concern.

"There was. Eleven of us."

Victor pulled up a stool and sat down. Yazpar turned from his almost-finished work and made himself comfortable. In a factual manner, Victor told of the garage dropping into a sink hole and the collapsing of the opening to the sink hole. Returning home wasn't an option. "We escaped into the mine shaft and the numerous tunnels leading nowhere."

"How terrible. You must have been terrified."

"More like relieved. We just escaped certain death."

Yazpar nodded with a slight smile.

"Then we found writings about Vanna, poems of Vanna. It sounded like…" He searched for an appropriate word.

"A heavenly place?" offered Yazpar.

"I was thinking of a resort, a place where we could have good times. But yeah, heavenly might be good too. Anyway, those poems gave us hope. Maybe we could find this Vanna. We could be with people again. It seemed our only chance."

"So where are the others?"

In a lowered voice he answered, "Dead. Accidents of one sort or another."

"Sorry to hear that."

Victor's mind shifted to Perry, then Terry, Graham, and Brayden. Yazpar's voice brought him back to the present.

"So, you guys wandered around in the tunnels?"

"Boy did we."

"Must have been depressing, going nowhere."

"That was the least of our problems." Victor shook his head. "If I were to believe Perry, I'd say—"

"Perry?"

"One of my best friends. On the way up here, he slipped and fell into the lake."

Yazpar nodded.

"Anyway, as I was saying, Perry believed the tunnels were inhabited by the devil."

Yazpar's eyes raised. "The devil! Because?"

"We were being picked off one by one."

Yazpar squinted.

"Calvin, another of my best friends, was the first to go. An absolutely wonderful guy."

Victor told of Calvin wanting to get to some cold water on the other side of a deep fissure so that he could have a cold compress for Arny's swollen ankle. Victor described Calvin's attempt to go around a fissure by going out on a ledge.

"The ledge gave way, and Calvin fell to his death."

Victor continued telling other stories about Calvin. The last story was of how Calvin boosted Perry's self-confidence to the degree that Perry finally asked, Jessie, Victor's sister, out on a date.

"Until then, he'd been intimidated by Jessie's strong will. You see, she hated guys with huge egos. She'd cut them down. Perry is the opposite. I mean, Perry was the opposite. A humble guy. Well maybe shy, but not the kind of person my sister would put down. Calvin knew that. Calvin knew the two would hit it off. He was right."

"Tell me more about Perry."

The question slipped past Victor like a gentle blowing breeze. Jessie held his attention or rather her daring spirit brought memories of being at home.

She never hesitated to challenge me, mom, or even dad. But she always did it in a questioning way. Her questions always showed she spoke after careful consideration. I'm never going to see her again.

"Victor?"

"Yes," replied Victor, refocusing.

"Tell me about Perry. You mentioned him earlier."

"Well, he was always trying to help others, and by others, I mean even those who weren't his close friends. You could count on him for a listening ear."

Stories about Perry stalled. Victor sat with a blank look on his face.

"Tell me about Perry and Mrs. Rashad," said Yazpar, deliberately mispronouncing the elderly lady's name.

"Mrs. Rastood," corrected Victor, refocusing.

Yazpar smiled and nodded in agreement.

Victor collected the facts and smiled. "Now *that* is a story that shows Perry listened. In a Community Caring course that he and Calvin took, they had visited Mrs. Rastood, a lonely lady in a nursing home. Their assignment over a portion of the course was to write a journal about a particular person. After Perry handed in his work, he continued to visit her.

"Mrs. Rastood had only two relatives in the city, an invalid sister who couldn't visit her, and her son. She was very proud of him, but he never visited her. Perry convinced a staff member to give him the contact information for the son. She wasn't supposed to. Anyway, Perry talked to the son. He found out the son thought his mother didn't want to have anything to do with him. She'd been very critical about how he spent or, in her words, how he *wasted* his money. Once the son found out his mother's true feelings, he began visiting his mother. Then Perry slowly reduced his visits.

"Sounds like Perry has a real heart."

That's what Perry said about Jessie, thought Victor.

"He did and—" He paused. "Excuse me." Victor stood up. "I have to—." He couldn't finish his thought—*I have to go, to be by myself. I need some privacy.*

Memories of Jessie demanded Victor's attention. Her laughter, her pranks, her .... Victor walked away afraid that Yazpar might see his tears.

Yazpar remained seated, observing his guest slowly shuffle to the spot where he had first found Victor curled up on the ground. Victor stopped and just stared into the sky. The usually alert Victor stood statue still even though a couple of birds flew very near him. Victor's head never turned.

Relief swept over Yazpar. The possibility that Victor might continue to walk into the wilderness didn't happen. Yazpar wouldn't have to try to find him. For a while, Yazpar watched what he sensed was a deeply troubled boy.

Yazpar went to the entrance of his living quarters and began preparing supper. Later, Victor walked up to him. Walked, not dragging his feet like he did when he stepped away earlier.

"Feeling better," said Yazpar conversationally without glancing up from his work.

"Some. I couldn't shake some thoughts." He paused. "Thoughts of my sister. It's like..."

He couldn't say the impression that slapped him. *Like she was dead. I'm never going to see her again.*

"Never mind," added Victor. He looked away, searching for a private spot.

"You really miss her."

Victor nodded, afraid how his voice might crack.

"So, you know what might help?" He glanced at Victor. Once he had Victor's attention, he continued, "A change of focus. I'd ask you to help prepare supper, but I'm almost done. I have another idea. You interested?"

"Why not," replied Victor.

Hearing Victor's normal tone, Yazpar asked, "Why not tell me about another one of your friends? Maybe Jean."

"Jean. Well, he was sort of a loner, a kind of quiet rebel."

"Interesting."

"I think what won our group's strong support for him was his sense of justice. He was also very courageous and determined. He first grabbed my attention when I learned he had quit a job at convenience store, one he liked very much. He said he liked his humorous, non-vulgar, easy going boss. Then he quit. No explanation."

Yazpar shook his head and continued with supper.

"Jean caught his boss ripping off a customer. Something about a discounted product being sold at full price. In private, Jean asked him about it. The boss excused his action by saying the customer could afford it. 'Wasn't fair,' Jean had said. 'Such a person can't be trusted. Never know when he will rip you off.' So, he quit. His parents were furious. Said he was looking for an excuse not to work. Said he was lazy. I admired him for his stand and told him so. After hearing what happened, a few other guys in our group supported him too. Our acceptance of him encouraged him to start hanging around with us."

"Man of integrity."

"Exactly. You know, once Jean found out about a couple of students who had stolen answers to a chem midterm. They were making a bundle selling them. The teacher didn't know about it until Jean reported the situation to him. Result— the midterm exam was cancelled, and the weight of the final was double. Lots of angry kids. Those who bought the answers got nothing for their money. No refunds. Those boys became the subject of some abuse too. Word leaked out that Jean had reported the cheating. Was he unpopular! Our group stood up for him. I think that convinced Jean that we really were his friends."

"Understandable." Yazpar served supper and each had a glass of his home-made blue-berry wine.

As Victor ate, he continued to talk about Jean. "That didn't change him. He still had a strong independent, loner mentality. That was probably why he lost his life."

Victor told Yazpar how Jean was convinced that tunnel B was the most direct route to Vanna. Even though the other guys didn't want to help with the digging, he began excavating by himself. He advanced quite a way before the tunnel collapsed on him.

"Perry led the memorial service for Jean, like he did for Calvin." Victor took another sip of the wine.

"Memorial service?"

"Well, kind of. We shared memories of our friend. Then Perry prayed asking that God would take Jean to heaven. He asked that for each of us, when one of us died. That way, once again we would be together. We always closed with the Lord's Prayer. We'd say it in unison. Saying it that way made us feel like..." He searched for a good explanation. "Like we were stronger, stronger because we were one."

A long silence settled over them. Then Yazpar quietly said, "You really miss your friends."

"I do. We were looking forward to being in Vanna together. Of having a good time there."

"Good time?"

"Yes, Arny read some kind of poems that described really good things that we could do."

"Like?"

IN THE END

"I can't remember exactly. I recall something about fishing, paddle boats."

"Ah yes," said Yazpar. He recited:

> Fishing, canoeing
> Paddleboats and water-skis
> My water-fun home

"Yes, that sounds like it. You know it?"

Victor's energized reaction painted a smile on Yazpar's face.

"I do. Many such poems were written praising Vanna." Laughing, he added, "I like the one about the fruit."

> Pears, cherries, apples,
> Raspberries and strawberries
> Gardener's delight"

Then raising his half empty glass of wine, he added, "And this."

Victor wondered how this old man knew so much about the journal poems. He was about to ask when Yazpar redirected his attention.

"Love cats?"

"Yeah," answered Victor, puzzled. *Where's this going?*

"Then you'll love this Vanna poem."

> My purring pussy
> modeling relaxation
> Vanna's essence."

Images of Candy came to Victor's mind. Candy, his sister's cat, was stretched out on the arm of the chesterfield. Wasn't supposed to be there, but no one had the heart to chase her off. She looked so peaceful.

"What a wonderful trait of Vanna," said Yazpar.

"What do you mean?"

"It's a place where you can be completely content, completely happy. No worries. Learn a new skill." He paused. "Like playing a musical instrument." He paused again to study Victor. "Say a guitar."

Victor grinned.

Yazpar nodded, knowing that was one of Victor's hopes. "And you're able to play, or watch, any game you want. Or be like the cat I once had and take a nap at any time of the day. Vanna's wonderful. Hey! I have a great idea. Let's toast Vanna."

The excitement in Yazpar's voice left Victor with no choice but to join him.

Yazpar raised his glass. "To a heavenly Vanna," he said. Their glasses clinked. "Drink up."

Victor took a long sip of the wine and pretended to enjoy the taste. Remembering Candy made him think of his sister. *I'll never see her again. Never.* He turned away from Yazpar so Yazpar wouldn't see his sense of loss. *Don't want to start talking about her.* His index finger went to his to brush away a tear that had fallen.

Yazpar noted Victor's changed demeanor. He refilled their glasses. Concerned that his reference to a cat may have brought a touch of despair, he redirected Victor's attention.

"Tell me about one of your other friends. Perhaps Sampson. He was a good friend of yours too. The one the others tended to follow a lot."

At the sound of his friend's name, Victor quickly turned around. *I never mentioned Sampson's name. Where'd he get that from?* Victor studied the old man for a moment. There was no changed expression like he was caught revealing something he shouldn't have. Victor reviewed the friends he'd been talking about. It struck him that he was talking a lot. *Could this wine be getting to me? Could I have already mentioned Sampson?*

"I understand he's very well liked."

"Was," corrected Victor. He took a long sip of wine, now enjoying its taste. "Sampson often provided some kind of direction for our group, mostly because he was usually on top of details. When we came to a split in the tunnels, Sampson recommended that we always make the same decision. Be easier to remember. He chose the right side. That was the kind of guy he was, always thinking ahead. We had no problem following him."

The more Victor talked, the more he drank. The more he drank the more he talked. Victor's stories switched to Sampson, their party organizer. "Sampson didn't let the forecast of a weekend of heavy rain dampen his spirits. He organized a party in his man cave. He often planned social events, golfing trips, or downhill skiing adventures for long weekends."

Stories about Sampson continued. So did the glasses of wine. By the end of the evening, Victor's spirits soared even though his body felt drained. That night, he slept very well.

Yazpar was up early, but Victor slept in. When he did wake up, all he wanted was some tea. An upset stomach checked his appetite and the day's ambitions. He sat out in the sun; eyes closed. He felt like he was tanning on a holiday.

Later, he accepted Yazpar's invitation to join him on a yoga workout and a walk to a small garden bed he had created.

"This is like a little oasis," said Victor, looking around at a patch of blueberry bushes. In a partially shaded area, short raspberry bushes grew. The berries weren't ripe yet.

Pointing to the area where the raspberry bushes were, Yazpar confessed he had to get the Catolone boys to bring up several bags of soil before those bushes took root. "When I water them, I get tasty fruit."

After a short time of weeding, Yazpar led Victor to a small stream where they filled up a few jugs of water and carried them back to their living quarters.

Victor returned to his tanning spot and slept for the rest of the afternoon. When he woke up, he saw a backpack and a bulging sack of artwork stacked near the entrance of the lodging. Yazpar explained he planned to go to Vanna next morning. He would sleep over at a friend's that night and then set up at his display at the farmer's market. He expected to sell most of his paintings.

"You'll love the place," said Yazpar. "It is better than you can possibly imagine."

While Victor was eating, Yazpar excused himself. "A small errand," he said. When he returned, Victor had finished supper.

Yazpar tossed Victor a loose-fitting burlap top to replace Victor's tattered T-shirt.

"No fashion statement," he said, picking up his glass of wine. "Looks better than what you're wearing. In Vanna, you'll find something more to your liking."

One of his, thought Victor. He changed reluctantly. *Too big.*

Victor's late climbing efforts still left him weak. He felt listless, tired. He hated that feeling. At the same time, he knew he'd lost interest in Vanna. It had little to offer him. Yazpar's excitement irritated him. It showed Victor he was out of step with reality, at least Yazpar's reality.

"Tomorrow will be a great day. I can hardly wait." Looking at Victor, he asked, "Excited?"

An unenthusiastic "yeah" came from Victor's lips.

"Hey. Why so glum? I thought this is what you were after. Going to Vanna. This is like going to heaven. Isn't that what you prowled around those dark tunnels for?"

"You don't get it." Anger tinted Victor's response. It was louder than he expected "There's no attraction in Vanna anymore."

"What do you mean? This is the place where you can to pursue your dearest passions, sports, creative activities, whatever. Remember, enjoying close personal relationships characterize Vanna." He recited a haiku that Perry read

> One large family.
> Everyone knows everyone.
> Close community.

"What else could you ask for?" He sipped his wine.

"My friends. They're gone. Activities don't matter. It's doing things with your friends that count. I have nothing to look forward to."

"It sounds like you'd be comfortable being dead so you could be with your friends in heaven."

Startled, Victor looked at Yazpar. *Is he reading my mind?* Victor said nothing.

"Tell me, didn't you say Perry lead the memorial service for each of your friends?"

"Yes."

"And that he asked God to take each of your friends to heaven?"

"Yes."

"So, you would be together?"

Victor nodded.

"Do you believe that?"

Victor nodded.

"Comforting." He paused. "Or is it?"

"What do you mean?"

"I believe you said the Vanna poems described an ideal place."

"So?"

"Ideal. Like heaven."

Victor said nothing.

"I mean, an ideal place sounds…" Yazpar paused until Victor looked up at him. "Heavenly."

"Never thought of it like that."

"And if Vanna is such an ideal place, wouldn't you have both, 'good things to do' *and* your friends?" He took a sip of wine while he carefully watched Victor's reaction.

Victor's blank expression suggested that Yazpar's possibility was too far-fetched.

"Before we leave, I thought you might like a bird's-eye view of Vanna, or at least a part of it. Interested?"

Victor said nothing.

"Come."

Puzzled, Victor followed his host. Their brisk fifteen-minute walk took them to a perch overlooking a valley. What spread out before them looked like a large European village. For a few minutes, Victor looked at what he'd guessed were parks, churches, the town's commercial center, and spacious treed residential areas with winding roads. Yazpar pointed to an area filled with glass boxed buildings. "Factories," he said.

Seeing a river running through three different lakes reminded Victor of another haiku line— paddleboats and water skis. *Oh boy.* "It looks so beautiful," Victor said softly.

"Wait until you are there at street level. The streets look like they are winding their way through parks. The public buildings are architectural wonders. The exterior design of people's houses suggests distinct personalities. Excited?"

"I wish all my friends could see this." His sadness returned.

"If that's the blessing you seek, don't be surprised to find them there too. Anything is possible." Yazpar's hand rested on Victor's shoulder.

"Really! If that's right, I can hardly wait to be there."

"Sounds like waiting until tomorrow would be waiting for a long time?"

"Yeah."

"I bet you wish you were there already."

"I do."

"Well, I believe I can help you with that," said Yazpar, as Victor's eyes were transfixed to the scene below.

"That would be great."

"Then so shall it be. I'll see you tomorrow."

Yazpar placed his hand on Victor's back and pushed.

Victor plunged over the cliff's edge. His scream echoed from the mountain on the opposite side of the valley.

Yazpar smiled.

CHAPTER 18

Epilogue

After supper, Yazpar rode a scooter to the Vanna Recovery Center. He'd timed his appearance to be shortly after Victor would regain consciousness. Before arriving, Yazpar sensed Victor had opened his eyes, met Agnes, his caregiver, and asked Agnes where he was. In response to her answer, Victor closed his eyes.

When Yazpar arrived at the recovery center, he thanked Agnes and told her to take an hour off. After Agnes left, he walked into Victor's room.

Victor turned to see who entered. *You! What are you doing here? Why did you push me off the cliff?* He turned away from Yazpar.

Yazpar read Victor's thoughts. He dragged a wooden chair up to his former guest's bed, deliberately making noise. Victor's disbelieving eyes turned in his direction.

"Welcome to your Vanna, your heaven on earth."

Victor's head pulled away from his visitor, sinking into his pillow. "You pushed me over the cliff."

With a smile, Yazpar said, "I'm fine thank you. And, how are you?

After a moment of assessment, Victor said, "Weak."

"In an hour or two, that will pass."

"Why'd you push me off the cliff?"

"Well, before we went for a bird's-eye view of Vanna, I sensed you'd be comfortable being dead so you could be with your friends in heaven. When I said that, the expression on your face told me I was right. Anyway, you did say you couldn't wait to get to Vanna." He sat straight back in the chair. "How do you feel?"

"Confused."

"But feeling no pain."

Victor said nothing.

"Even after a fall like you took."

Victor's expression remained unchanged.

"That's what you believe, isn't it? There's no pain in heaven?"

Victor's skepticism continued.

"Didn't you tell me that when each of your friends died, you prayed that they would meet in heaven?

"Yes."

"So, if you were to meet one of those friends now, you would believe that you are in heaven?"

Victor said nothing.

Yazpar waited. "Well?"

"I think so."

"Good. Because Perry is waiting for you in the next room. I sense he's growing quite anxious to see you."

Victor said nothing.

"In that case, if there is nothing else, I should be leaving." Yazpar stood up.

"Wait."

Victor's plea forced Yazpar to sit down. When Victor said nothing, Yazpar said, "You have questions for me?"

"You pushed me over the cliff. You tried to kill me. Why?"

"Hmmm…'tried.' Must mean you see yourself as alive. Good. As for killing you, I couldn't. You were already dead. I just nudged you toward your heavenly Vanna, the heaven you looked forward to."

"What?" Victor paused, surprised at the energy in his voice. "You make no sense." Moving to a sitting position on his bed, Victor said, "Who are you? Or rather, what are you?"

"What do you think?"

"I don't know. You seem to know things. Things I haven't told you. At times, you knew my thoughts. You seemed to be looking out for me like—" He paused to grasp for an appropriate description. "Like some kind of guardian angel? Is that what you are?"

"More like a comforter. At least that's my role. I haven't fully transitioned to my eternal calling."

"Eternal calling?"

"My goal is to be one who welcomes people to their concept of what heaven would be like. It's a stepping-stone on the way to eternal heaven. There are times my energy is drained. I slip back to a more human existence."

"You comfort?"

"Yes. When the garage you talked about dropped into the sink hole, I was sent to comfort you and your friends and to escort all of you to heaven. At first, I thought *an easy job*. I expected after the garage hit the bottom of the sinkhole, your bodies would stop functioning. I would be there to remind you of your belief in heaven and lead you to your Vanna. That would be normal. But the garage didn't plunge down right away. After the second short drop, Calvin had lowered himself down the sinkhole and found an old mine shaft. *A possible escape area,* you all thought. Through Sampson's planning, you and your friends were prepared to make good your escape."

"I remember all that," said Victor, making himself more comfortable on the bed.

"Then the garage dropped again."

"Because we had gathered around the hole in the floor?"

"No. Because the rocks, or pins, as Sampson had called them, lost their hold. This time the drop was greater. The garage walls caved in. I read your feelings, your panic. You all knew death was close. None of you were ready for that. You all had the same reaction—refuse to accept death. It was like you thought you could do something about that. Emotions ran wild. It was like you felt you were at the doorstep of hell. *We're going to die. We can't die. I'm too young to die. I won't escape. Can't be.*

"I hadn't experienced my charges in such turmoil before. Those screams, so many of those screams. They almost drowned out the sound of a huge chunk of the cement floor that hit the bottom of the sinkhole. Of course, no one heard your screams for help except me. Such tension. It hardly seemed a fitting mood to enter your Vanna.

"I felt something had to be done. On my own, I made a decision. I'd comfort you. Provide you with a calming spirit. A coping spirit. A chance to recall that death was not the end. A chance to remember that heaven awaited you. An opportunity to anticipate a place of everlasting joy and what that might be like."

"Wait a minute. I don't remember any of this. Sure, we were really scared. Anyone would be."

"That's right. I replaced that moment of terror with the vision of your escape, just as you guys had planned. By choosing to preserve and redirect your conscious spirit, I adjusted the passage of time so I could work with you, to help you boys to adapt from the hell you saw before you, to the joy of being in heaven. You had time for you to clarify what was really important in life. Your new temporary experience meant stimulating your imagination. That way you could feel like you succeeded in escaping to the mine's tunnels. I thought I could pull it off. I had already sensed the feelings of hope and fear about being lowered down to the mine shaft. That was my starting point. From there I made your new realities. Then I utilized your curiosity to begin your exploration of the tunnels. You were totally focused on your new environment. You were calm. I succeeded. I had to. That was all you had left. Your bodies were being hurled down. Soon they'd strike solid rock."

"We're dead!"

"Only physically. When you experienced the borrowed time with your friends, no. You hadn't hit the bottom of the sinkhole.'

"But some of us spent days in the tunnels." Victor shook his head in disbelief.

"True. I redirected you to a different time reality from earthly time to heaven's timelessness. In a matter of seconds, you experienced a special time with your friends, something your premature death was taking away from you. Because you couldn't accept your own death, through your imagination, I gave you a chance to be with each other a little longer. It was what you wanted. I was there for you. I gave you areas to explore—the tunnels, mountainside scenes, the lake. The Vanna journals gave you a concrete goal to work toward."

Victor's brow wrinkled. "But then we started dying?"

"Well, leaving the group," corrected Yazpar.

"That's not what we wanted."

"Yes. That wasn't in my plans either, but that *is* what each of you wanted. For a few moments at least, you entered your own private world, one you were very comfortable with. Thanks to Calvin, I learned that. You all had strong, independent natures. Perhaps that's why you bonded so well. When Calvin stepped out on the ledge, his thoughts were centered on Arny, caring for Arny. He wasn't thinking about being with the group. This is what he saw heaven was like—people caring for people. It's what he looked forward to. By caring for Arny, he was already trying to live that new temporary reality that each of you imagine. He knew venturing out on the ledge was dangerous, but he wasn't afraid. After he hit the bottom of the crevice, I was there for him. I pointed out that his love for Arny is just the kind of person God loves. He'd be a ready fit for heaven. He was willing to come with me to heaven."

"Then Perry's prayer was answered. Calvin was taken to heaven."

"Yes."

"But what about Jean? He wasn't trying to help anyone."

"Actually, he was motivated by wanting to help the whole group. Everyone's interest in finding Vanna convinced him that if he could find a faster route there, everyone would be happy. He'd have been a big help. I sensed he was also motivated by a guilt, like he hadn't done anything to deserve the group's respect. He seemed to feel he didn't really fit in with the group."

"There was no requirement to be part of the group. Just join us whenever you could. That's all." Victor shook his head.

"Be that as it may, Jean was so convinced that he knew the best way to Vanna, that he didn't hesitate to follow his own path. He didn't have to work with the group to rescue them. Once he began his excavating, he was in his own world. This is how he saw heaven as being. He didn't have to worry about what the group may say if he walked his own path. Fear of death didn't exist. His willingness to clear a route to Vanna made it possible for me to show him that he was a loving person, what others in heaven would rejoice over. When I promised him that the rest of the group would eventually see him there, he relaxed. His spirt was calm. He agreed to come with me."

"Calm spirit. You're saying that we're restless spirits?" Victor's brow furrowed.

"Not so much restless as needy. I sensed the group was the source of happiness, or safety or both. I'm not really sure which. As long as there was a desire to cling to the group, no one would leave it. There wouldn't be peace. You wouldn't be able to come to the heaven you had hoped for. That meant I needed to be there for you. By giving your group a common goal to strive toward, you felt comfortable. Finding Vanna was that goal. Exploring the tunnels was a means of getting there, something you could do together."

"But that wasn't always our number one goal."

"You're right. And Len and Larry are a good example. I thought for sure that they would always stay with your group. But it appeared they were equally happy being with each other. Their shared love of food and competing with each other refocused their attention—who wins the race? Who gets the hot dog? This what they looked forward to in their heavenly Vanna. There was no hint of tension. No worry. Falling to their death was the furthest thing from their minds. After their fall, I pointed to their caring relationship for each other to show them that they were ready to be in heaven. No hesitation. They accepted."

For a moment, Yazpar chuckled.

"What?" asked Victor.

"I came to visit them, like I am with you. Know what the first thing Larry asked for?"

Victor shook his head.

"Anywhere close by where a guy can grab a hot dog or burger? I told them where they could go after they had sufficiently transitioned."

"What about Arny?"

"Arny too, had his thoughts redirected. He imagined seeing an old girlfriend. You wouldn't know her. He'd met her at a church conference. They communicated over the phone and Skype for almost a year. Then she died in a car accident. It hit him hard. You may remember there was a month that he didn't show up for your group gatherings."

"That was just last year."

"Yes. He still thought of her. He didn't tell anyone except his mother. He was afraid of being seen as too sentimental. So, fear of drowning after diving into the lake was the furthest thing from his mind.

He just wanted to be with her. This what his heavenly Vanna would give him."

"What about Perry? Before he died, there wasn't much of a group to hang around with."

"Ah-h-h-h, Perry. He sure hated those tunnels. Being out in the open with you was like heaven to him. What was almost equally important was being with you. Your relationship with him was so strong that it countered being with the whole group. Separating the two of you was hard. The climb that he took to rescue you when you climbed the tower gave him new confidence. His fear of falling diminished. That is why he had no concerns about walking along the cliff's edge by the lake. He loved looking down at it. And when you stood on the peak above him, he could see himself climbing up the sharp incline to you. He could even see himself climbing up from the lakeshore too. Fear was gone. To him, he was already living a heavenly Vanna. He knew what his heavenly Vanna would have. That was my time to bring him home."

Victor took a breath to ask a question but didn't say anything. Yazpar waited.

After a long silence, Victor looked at Yazpar and said, "You may not know this, but often Perry sensed another presence when we were in the tunnels. Do you know anything about that?"

"Yes. That was me he sensed. He was very spiritually sensitive."

"You were the devil?"

"In his mind, yes. He first noticed my presence after he had returned to the sinkhole to finish working on his map and also when Jean died. That wasn't a problem. Then I created the impression of the tunnel cave-in, eliminating a possible rescue route. His strong sense of fear made him expect the worst. He suspected only the devil would do such a thing. The devil was on the hunt. Instead of me being a source of comfort, I was a source of tension. I had to keep my distance from him."

"If Perry was with us, you couldn't be near us. We were safe from you manipulating our minds."

At the sound of "manipulate," Yazpar flinched. He hoped he was coming across as a helper, not someone who was doing something for his own benefit.

"You're right. But if I kept my distance, it made it hard for me to read the thoughts and feelings of the boys. It made it hard to create the next experience that they would be comfortable facing. That's why Len and Larry, and later Arny, were able to take off on their own adventures. When I caught up with them, I had to work with whatever was in their minds."

"Hold it. After Perry fell into the lake, didn't you come to him?"

"Yes, but—"

"And you think that made him feel comfortable?" Victor sat up, ready to poke his finger in Yazpar's chest.

"No, which is why I had to contact him in a different way. I knew after we left the tunnels his fear had subsided. So did his sharp sense of defense.

But I didn't know if my presence would trigger his fear again. I didn't want that. Fear distorts peace and common sense. I chose to not to reveal myself physically, but I gave him the impression of my presence. That almost didn't work. He immediately suspected I, as the devil, had caused his foot to fall and him to tumble down into the lake. I sent him images of me talking with Calvin and Jean and the others. It calmed him down. He recognized the purpose of my visit. His only question was if you would be coming to heaven too. I said yes. He eagerly went with me. He looked forward to seeing the rest of his friends."

"Wait a minute." Anger raised the volume of Victor's response. "This makes no sense."

"Why?"

"You said that as long as we needed to hang on to the feeling of being together, you were there for us."

"Yes. I was waiting until you were at peace and able to come to the heaven you had hoped for."

"And that was the case for each of us?"

Yazpar explained his presence for the death of each of Victor's other friends. Yazpar sat watching Victor. He sensed Victor's reluctance to ask a question. "So, are you going to ask me something?"

"About what?" asked Victor.

"What about yourself?"

"Okay. What about me? There was no group left for me to be attached to. There was no need for you to hang around."

"But you weren't at peace. I had to wait until you would be comfortable going to heaven."

"Why did I have to go through all of that—" He paused, not knowing what to call his experience.

"You were the most difficult boy. You have such a very strong will. Nothing was going to get the better of you. You met the tunnel challenges, climbed the tower, and walked to my quarters. You intended to do whatever it took to find Vanna. You expected to be taxed to the maximum. I sensed you thought that if Vanna was easy to find, it wouldn't be worth it. Also, you had to demonstrate that you were unstoppable, a person deserving to be a resident of Vanna. Like Jean, you felt you had to earn your acceptance. What surprised me was that you continued to climb to the top of the summit. At one point during your mourning for Perry, you thought his death was your fault. Do you remember?"

Victor looked uncertain.

"Your thoughts went something like '*What was so important about Vanna anyway? An ideal community. Big deal. How ideal could it be without all my friends?*' You appeared to dismiss the importance of Vanna. I expected you to return to the lake where Brayden, Graham, and Terry died. The extra day that you and Perry stayed there was a time of peace for both of you. I planned to return to you when you reached the lake. I certainly didn't expect to see you looking down from the summit at my shelter."

"It was tempting," admitted Victor, "but I don't like abandoning a goal."

"As I surmised," said Yazpar. "Then you surprised me again. When you learned that Vanna was at hand, you no longer cared for it. You still weren't at peace. I felt like your father."

"My father?"

"Yes. Do you remember when you joined the reserves?"

Victor nodded.

"Your father was surprised that you were giving up on being with your family and friends. He thought those were the most important things in your life. How could you give all that up? When you returned after the first term of training, he realized that you had figured it out. You knew friends and family was what really brought you joy. You wouldn't be returning for another year. Being yourself meant being with those who accepted you as you were, who trusted you, who loved you.

"In the end, I saw you had figured it out. In addition to seeing Vanna as a place of safety, you also needed the hope of being with your friends. When I told you that you would see your group, your fear of being alone evaporated. Peace returned to you. What really excited you was hearing you could look forward to going fishing with Uncle Bob."

"I never thought of that kind of possibility."

"I know. I remember your response. 'I'll see Uncle Bob?' I wish you could've seen the expression on your face when I said, 'Of course. He's looking forward to being with you too.' That's memorable! I also told you when you're ready, you'll see other members of your family. That's what heaven is about. Being with friends and family, one of the ingredients to a joyful life. That's your heavenly Vanna, at least until the final day comes.'"

Yazpar waited for several minutes. "Well? No other questions?"

The silence was short.

"We could have walked down to Vanna together."

"Not my choice. My assignment meant you had to experience the end of your old life. That door had to be closed. In the end, your blessing is that when you open the next door to your new life, you have a bit of an idea of what awaits you. In your case, you knew a little more. You had a peak at Vanna. Anything else?"

Victor shook his head.

"Good. Because Perry is waiting in the next room. We've been in here so long I think he is afraid you don't want to see him."

Yazpar faced the door expecting someone to enter. Victor looked too.

The door opened.

"Perry." Victor's response was so low that one would expect he didn't want anyone to hear him say something that he thought was impossible.

Yazpar got out of his chair to make way for Perry.

"Hi, old buddy." Perry came up and gave a high five to his friend.

"Is that really you?"

"In the flesh. I'm so glad to see you. Our prayers are answered. We have been fully restored."

"That's hard to believe."

"Believe it. And here's something else you will find hard to believe. Remember how scared Brayden was about swimming?"

Victor nodded.

"Well, he's swimming now. And loving it." Perry saw a slight smile but no sign of surprise. "Something wrong?"

"Probably nothing. Lately things have not been what they've seemed to be. Hope you don't mind, but I'd like to ask you a few questions."

"Fire away."

Victor asked Perry some things that only he and Perry would know. Perry's answers began with his fall into the lake, and then they went to some stories that he and Victor shared at school. Yazpar nodded and smiled as the boys talked.

"We can continue talking for some time," said Perry. "But first I feel we should let Yazpar say his goodbye. I sense he still has something important to share with you."

"Sense?"

Yazpar approached the bed.

Yazpar read Victor's surprise. "You're very obser-vant. Like Sampson. You're right. Perry said *sense*. I did too. It's a kind of mind reading, a sending of images that express feeling. We've developed it over short distances so that we could better understand each other. You'll see. There are no doubt other things or skills that you have always wanted to do. Now that's possible. Sampson had the same reaction as you have."

"Sampson?"

"Yes, Sampson will be here. Probably within an hour. He was singing. He was in the middle of recording a song he composed. It was a dream he'd often privately toyed with. I've contacted all your other friends. They'll be here tomorrow. You'll see that you are truly blessed. Then you can thank God for your faith."

Note from author:

Did you enjoy reading In the End?

Your feedback helps me provide the best quality books and helps other readers like you discover great books.

Is there anything you find memorable about any of the characters or what they did or saw?

It would mean the world to me if you took two minutes to share your thoughts about this book as a review. You can leave a review on the retailer of your choice and/or send me an email with your honest feedback.

Do you know of anyone else for whom this book would be a good fit?

Thanks
Ken
My e-mail address is:
callingkensaik@gmail.com

CPSIA information can be obtained
at www.ICGtesting.com
Printed in the USA
BVHW041851010521
606241BV00007B/8